The blonde cried "MURDER"

She swore that she had found her brother murdered in a waterfront hotel, his throat slit from ear to ear. And Mike believed her—even though the corpse had vanished, even though a strange young man appeared and identified himself as the supposed victim.

Once again, Shayne's weakness for a gorgeous woman involved him in murder. Only this time he had to find the corpse before he could find the killer.

"BRISK AND VIOLENT"
—San Francisco Chronicle

WELL OVER TWENTY-FIVE MILLION OF MIKE SHAYNE MYSTERIES HAVE BEEN PRINTED IN DELL BOOK EDITIONS ALONE.

THE
BLONDE
CRIED
MURDER

BRETT HALLIDAY

A DELL MYSTERY

Published by
DELL PUBLISHING COMPANY, INC.
750 Third Avenue
New York 17, N.Y.

Reprinted by arrangement with the author

Dedicated to:
David and Helen Kasson. With
sincere thanks for the helping
hand they gave toward the
writing of this book

Previous Dell Edition: #946

New Dell Edition
First printing—September, 1963

Printed in Canada

ONE: *9:32 P.M.*

Evelyn Thompson yawned not too prettily as she lounged in front of the switchboard at the Hibiscus Hotel. Normally she was quite a pretty girl, but tonight her face was sullen, her lips pouting with discontent.

Still two and a half hours until midnight! Roger wouldn't wait. She knew darned well he wouldn't. Not for two whole hours. And there wasn't a chance in the world to get in touch with him and explain that things had gone haywire, that the other operator, who'd promised faithfully just that afternoon to relieve Evelyn at ten, so she could keep her date, had called up a while ago to say she had a headache and couldn't make it tonight.

A headache? Haw! And her voice all blurry with gin. Wait until she asked Evelyn for a similar favor. Just wait! That's all.

Evelyn yawned again and patted her open mouth delicately with flame-tipped fingers. Wouldn't be so bad if there was anything doing, but after nine o'clock at night at the Hibiscus in the off-season it was like running a switchboard in a morgue. Maybe there'd be half a dozen calls from partying rooms upstairs for more ice and soda before she went off at midnight. And that'd be all. For that, Evelyn had to sit here and miss her date with Roger.

And he'd be sore as the devil about it. This was distinctly not the proper point in her relationship with Roger to keep him waiting two hours with no explanation at all. She'd worked it so carefully up to now. Playing him along just enough—giving in to him a little more each date, but withdrawing into dignity just in time so now she really did have him all hot and bothered and worked up to the point where tonight—

A light flashed on the board in front of her. She stopped yawning and sat a little more erect and leaned forward negligently to plug in the connection. Room 360. That was Mr. Drood. "Drooling Drood," they called him. Not that he was so bad, but he did sort of seem to drool when he looked at a girl. Because his face was puffy and pink and always sweaty, and his full lips always looked wet.

Funny he should be calling down now. Only twenty minutes ago that Miss Payne in 414 had called him from her room. Evelyn had listened in, of course. Sometimes you heard some real good stuff when the guests of different sexes called each other late in the evening. And she'd seen that affair shaping up the last few days, too. Miss Payne was tall and had a sort of haughty way about her, but with a welcoming eye for the men for all that. Funny how she couldn't do better than old Drood. But then she was plenty old, too. Thirty-five at the least. And when you got that old, Evelyn thought complacently from her point of vantage at nineteen, you were just about ready to take anything that wore pants.

But they'd been very circumspect on that earlier call. Almost like they might have some idea a girl downstairs on the switchboard wouldn't have anything better to do than listen in, Evelyn told herself indignantly.

Just Miss Payne saying she'd found that piece in the paper she'd told Mr. Drood about that afternoon, and would he care to come up and get it? And Mr. Drood drooling into the phone how he'd love to, and maybe Miss Payne'd like it if he brought along a night-cap for the two of them. And Miss Payne saying she had the ice if he had anything to go along with it.

That was it, Evelyn told herself as the plug went in. No ice had gone up to 414 since about five o'clock. Probably she just had a couple of half-melted cubes left, and when they decided to stretch the night-cap out into another one, old Drood had slipped back to his own room to order it— as if that was going to fool anybody in a hotel.

Into the mouthpiece beneath her chin, Evelyn Thompson said in dulcet tones, "Your call, please?"

A woman's voice answered from 360. Panting and strained, hoarsely hysterical: "There's a dead man in three-sixteen. He's murdered. Oh, please hurry." And there was a click that closed the connection.

Evelyn sat rigid, staring at the board with dilated eyes. But that was Mr. Drood's room. 360. It *was* plugged into 360. Her staring eyes verified that fact. Sounded like the woman said "three-sixteen." But it was 360. Sure it was. She must have heard wrong.

Murder?

Evelyn frantically tried to call the number back. There was no answer. She jerked her head sidewise toward the profile of the clerk, half-dozing behind his desk, and whispered loudly, "Dick."

The profile stirred and the clerk's head turned languidly toward her. She motioned excitedly with one hand while she plugged in another connection.

The telephone buzzed in a private office behind the front desk, and a man who was dozing, fully clothed, on an old sofa in the small office slowly came to life.

Oliver Patton, "Chief Security Officer" of the Hibiscus, swung his feet over the edge of the sofa and sat up, rubbing his eyes. His was a twenty-four-hour job since he was the only dick the hotel afforded, and he had to catch his sleep when he could. Generally it wasn't bad. Most nights went straight through without requiring his services at all.

He yawned as he glanced at his watch and reached for the phone beside the sofa. He was a big man who had gone steadily to fat since retiring from the police force a few years ago. His bunions bothered him a good deal, but, with his wife's hospital bills, his pension simply wasn't enough and he needed this extra money.

Evelyn's low-pitched but excited voice leaped out of the receiver at him as he lifted it, "Trouble in three-sixty, Mr. Patton!"

"What kind of trouble?" he grunted sourly. "That's Drood, ain't it?"

"But it wasn't Mr. Drood. Some woman called. There's a dead man there."

"Dead?" Oliver Patton stopped scratching the fold of fat in front of his belly and his mouth gaped. "Drood?"

"I don't know. It's awful, Mr. Patton. You better get up there quick. She said murder. Should I call the police?"

"Murder?" Patton's voice took on a sharp note of authority. "Don't call anybody." He slammed down the phone and rose to his six feet two, his heavy face worried.

Murder in a hotel was real trouble. It was his job to keep the police out if there was any way possible. Of course, if it was murder, it wouldn't be possible. But he knew most of the boys on Homicide. Sometimes you could fix things so there wouldn't have to be any publicity.

He hurried out of his office and around a corner into the lobby where the clerk and bell-captain and elevator operator were grouped at the desk talking excitedly to Evelyn.

They all stopped talking and looked to him for advice as he came up with ponderous swiftness. He disregarded them and demanded of Evelyn, "What you got, girl?"

"Just that. A woman called from three-sixty and said there was a murdered man there. She hung right up on me and didn't answer when I called back."

"Come along, Bill," he snapped at the bell-captain. "You watch it here, Dick. Don't let anybody out—nobody up." He trotted heavily to the waiting elevator, and when the door slammed shut, asked the operator, "Bring anybody down recently?"

"They was a lady a few minutes ago, Chief. She come from five." As the elevator stopped and he opened the doors, he asked anxiously, "What must I do?"

"Hold it right here." snapped Patton. "No matter how many bells ring." He turned to his left with Bill at his heels, moved swiftly but quietly toward a door standing open with light streaming out of it.

The open door was numbered 360. The overhead lights were on, revealing an impersonal hotel bedroom with a double bed in the corner between two windows.

There was no woman in the room, and no dead man in sight. Everything was in perfect order with a man's bedroom slippers showing from under the bed, a pair of violently flowered pajamas lying across the foot of it, a set of silver-backed brushes on the dressing-table.

Patton stopped just inside the open door for a full thirty seconds while he surveyed the seemingly empty room, then motioned for Bill to remain behind while he crossed to the closed bathroom door and jerked it open. He switched on the inside light and found it empty. He turned to the single closet in the room and opened that door. Half a dozen light suits and jackets were on hangers in perfect order. No one was concealed behind them.

Patton turned about with a puzzled frown, shaking his head dubiously at the bell-captain in the doorway, then dropped to his knees beside the bed, lifted the trailing coverlet to look beneath it carefully.

He got to his feet, brushing off his knees, his eyes hard and probing as he swept up the telephone from the small table at the head of the bed.

He rumbled, "Have you gone nuts, Evelyn? There's no one here—alive or dead."

"But that's what she *said*. That there was a dead man. Murdered, she said. I can't help it, Mr. Patton, if—"

He growled, "Skip it. Tell me this. Drood supposed to be in?"

"He—" she faltered. "Well, he was in earlier. But—uh—four-fourteen called down to his room about half an hour ago."

Patton got a handkerchief from his pocket and wiped sweat from his face. "Who's four-fourteen?"

"Miss Payne."

"Tall and skinny?" he ruminated, blinking his eyes in thought. "He go up there?"

"Well, I— How should I know? I connected them and—"

"And listened in," he cut her short wearily. "Yes or no?"

"Well, yes. I guess maybe he did. I just happened to hear her ask him—"

"Okay, okay. Tell Dick to hold the fort while we take a look."

He shrugged at Bill as he replaced the phone. "Up in four-fourteen? You had anything here or there this evening?"

"Not since about six. Ice to Miss Payne."

Patton left the door standing open and the light burning as he led the way back to the elevator. The operator stood in the open door waiting for them anxiously.

The buzzer let out a long peal as they stepped in and he said, "Up one floor."

"Somebody on eight getting mighty mad," said the operator. "Was he plumb dead, Chief?"

"Not even half," said Patton disgustedly. "Let eight keep on being mad."

They turned to the right this time they left the elevator, went about twenty paces and turned left into an intersecting corridor. A dim, red exit light glowed at the end of the corridor marking the fire-stairs.

Patton stopped in front of the fourth door on the left, stenciled 414. Light came through the transom above the door.

He knocked rather loudly. The transom was closed and they could hear nothing from inside the room.

Patton waited ten seconds and knocked again. Then he rattled the knob. A frightened female voice came faintly through the wood. "Who is it?"

"Hotel detective. Open up, Miss Payne."

"I don't— How dare you?" The voice was louder and more indignant. "Go away from my door."

He rattled the knob again and put his mouth close to the wood. "You don't want to cause a lot of attention, Miss Payne. Neither do I. Unlock the door or I'll use my pass-key."

He waited grimly, and after an interval of fifteen or twenty seconds the door opened reluctantly.

He pushed it and strode into a bedroom that was not quite as orderly as the one they had just visited on the floor below. Miss Payne was shoved back by his entrance, still clinging to the knob.

She was tall and slender, with aquiline features and a somewhat sharp nose, and with lightly graying hair piled atop her head. Her dark eyes flashed angrily at the hotel detective, and she clutched a dark blue, tailored dressing gown tightly about her in front.

"How dare you?" she gasped. "What is the meaning of this—?"

"I'm looking for Mr. Drood," said Patton quietly, his glance going beyond her. The room was somewhat larger than 360, with two wide windows directly behind the bed. Their curtains billowed in the breeze that swept in from Biscayne Bay, just in front of the hotel.

The bed was neatly made up, and there was no sign of Drood's presence—unless you counted the pitcher of almost melted ice, the bottles of gin, and Tom Collins mix, and the two highball glasses standing sociably side by side on a table at the other end of the room.

"Mr. Drood? Indeed?" Miss Payne had a thin, unpleasantly high voice. She tossed her head in regal anger. "The absolute insolence—"

"Now, take it easy, Miss Payne." Patton held up a beefy hand to ward off her anger. "This ain't what you think. No harm in a couple of guests having a little drink together long's they don't bother other people. The management wants you to be happy here. But this is something else. I just had a dead man reported in Mr. Drood's room."

He raised his voice somewhat as he said this, and after a moment the tightly closed closet door opened and a portly, middle-aged man stepped out. He was in his shirt sleeves, but wearing a neat bow tie, his shiny face was wet with sweat and his thick lips were opening and shutting like a fish freshly taken from the water.

His eyes were round and frightened, and after several tries he managed to say, "A dead man, sir? In *my* room?"

"That was the report we got. How long you been here?"

Mr Drood drooled a trifle as he glanced despairingly at the haughtily silent Miss Payne, and he said humbly and weakly, "Perhaps half an hour. I just dropped in to—ah—to see an article of interest in the paper Miss Payne and I had discussed, and she was kind enough to—ah—offer me a refreshing drink." He waved with attempted nonchalance toward the glasses on the table.

"Neither of you been back to three-sixty since you came up?"

They both shook their heads and said, "No," simultaneously and distinctly.

"And you don't know anything about any dead man in your room, Mr. Drood?"

"Indeed not. I should never allow—that is—ah—*no*. Is this the truth?"

Patton shrugged. "Some kind of crazy hoax, I guess. Did you leave the door of your room unlocked when you came out?"

"I believe perhaps I did. Yes." Drood nodded anxiously. "Indeed, I believe I may have even left the door open. I expected to be gone just a moment, you see, and then,

when I arrived, Miss Payne was kind enough to—ah—"
Again he waved toward the drinks.

"Some drunk must have stepped in while you were out
and made the call. Well, can't blame you for that. Go
ahead and enjoy yourselves, folks. Sorry to've intruded,
but I had to check up."

"Of course you did, Officer. Naturally. We understand
perfectly." Drood was very effusive as they went out, but
Miss Payne did not echo his heartiness. She stood stiffly
and disdainfully aside, and closed the door hard the moment they were out in the hall.

"What do you make of it, Ollie?" asked Bill curiously
as they went back to the elevator. "Just a practical joke?"

"What else can I make of it? So long as we don't have a
body—"

The elevator buzzer was sounding insistently as they
re-entered it. Patton said, "Take us all the way down,
Joe. Then go ahead as usual. Tell 'em you've been out of
order for ten minutes."

In the lobby, he strode angrily around behind the desk
to confront Evelyn who started to jerk out questions as
he approached.

He held up a hand to cut her off and rumbled, "What
sort of tricks you pulling, Evvie?"

"No sort of tricks." Her eyes rounded. "Who was it?"

"Nobody." He stood in front of her flat-footed, both
hands on his hips, and his bunions hurt like the devil. "Not
a soul in the room. Drood all cozy with gin and sin upstairs in four-fourteen. You answer me that."

"But the call *did* come from three-sixty, Mr. Patton. I
swear it did. I left my plug in just to be sure and I
checked."

"Then you musta misunderstood what was said."

"No, I—I—" Slowly Evelyn's mouth widened into a big
round O. "I wonder. Gee, gosh, I wonder, Mr. Patton. I'll
tell you. When she first said: 'There's a dead man in,' I

thought she said in 'three-sixteen.' That's why I checked
my plug so careful and tried to call her back. But the call
was from three-sixty, so I just thought for sure I'd been
mistaken. I thought she must've said three-sixty instead of
three-sixteen because that's where the call came from.
Golly, do you suppose—?"

"Here we go again," said Patton sourly. "Three-sixteen,
huh? Who's three-sixteen, Dick?" he called to the clerk.

"U-m-m, that's Miss Paulson, I think. Yeh. Cute little
trick."

"She in now? Buzz her, Evvie," Patton added to the girl
in front of him.

Dick said, "I don't think—no. Her key's in the box. And
I think I remember seeing her go out a little while back."

"She doesn't answer," said Evelyn.

Oliver Patton shrugged. "Yeh. Well—you still think
maybe the call said three-sixteen instead of three-sixty?"

"Seems to me I'm sure of it now, the more I think back."

Patton turned away from her tiredly and went back to
the elevator, shaking his head at Bill this time. "Just to
double-check," he said.

When he reached the third floor again, he grimaced at
the door of 360 still standing open, and turned the other
way, as he had on the floor above, and into the corridor
leading to the left.

He stopped in front of the fifth door on his left this
time, 316, near the end of the corridor. The overhead
light was dim at this point, and no light showed through
the transom of this room.

Patton knocked loudly, waited and knocked again, or-
dering gruffly, "Open up or I'll use my pass-key."

When nothing happened, he got out a ring of keys,
selected one and unlocked the door. He stood on the
threshold and reached inside for the wall switch. He
blinked as the lights came up in a replica of Miss Payne's
room.

The interior was neat and a little warm because the windows beyond the bed, overlooking the bay, were closed. He entered stolidly and went through the motions of checking the room. He found nothing at all out of order, and left in a few minutes.

Returning to the elevator, he glared at the open door of 360 as he waited for a car. Now his feet were hurting so badly he'd have to soak them in hot water before getting back to sleep.

TWO: *9:37 P.M.*

A narrow alley runs beside the Hibiscus Hotel from the street in front to the stone breakwater at the rear of the ten-story building. It is used only by delivery and garbage trucks which must back in between the hotel and the brick apartment house on the other side of the alley.

At night, even when there is a full moon, there is black darkness at the bottom of the narrow slit between the two tall buildings. On this night there was only a sickle moon in the sky.

The running girl stumbled as she emerged suddenly from the blackness of the alley onto the lighted sidewalk. As she went down on both hands and one knee, she threw a terrified glance back into the alley behind her. She could see nothing, but she distinctly heard the running footsteps pursuing her.

Absolute terror mingled with hysteria to distort her features in a grimace of horror. She was on her feet instantly, running wildly along the sidewalk away from the lighted hotel entrance, like any hunted thing instinctively seeking safety in the darker shadows.

The headlights of a car on the street behind her picked up her fleeing figure. At the same moment a running man slid to a stop on the sidewalk at the spot where she had fallen. He looked quickly in both directions as the car drew abreast of him, saw her in flight half a block away and started in pursuit.

She looked over her shoulder once, saw the onrushing

car and the man just behind it. Her breath was coming in labored gasps and her heart was pumping wildly. She realized there was only one possible chance of escape. She whirled off the sidewalk directly in front of the fast-coming headlights, waving her arms frantically above her head, standing resolutely at a point where she would be run down if the driver did not stop.

There was the blat of a horn and the angry scream of brakes. Fortunately the brakes were good and they held on the dry pavement. The car lurched to a stop with its bumper inches from the girl's knees.

It was a taxi without the signal lights that would have indicated it was cruising empty. The uniformed driver leaned out angrily to shout at the frightened girl, but she darted around the left headlight to claw open the rear door, gasping, "Please go on—*fast.* Please, *please.*"

She was inside and slammed the door shut. The driver turned his head to argue with her, but her fist pounded on his shoulder as she sobbed out, "Go *on!* Before he gets here. Can't you see—?"

The driver could see she was young and beautiful and terrified. He also saw through the rear window the figure of the running man on the sidewalk behind them. He grunted sourly and threw the taxi in second and stepped on the gas. When the car leaped forward it threw the girl back against the rear cushion. Only at that moment did she become aware of the other passenger in the right-hand corner beside her—a woman, sitting very erect and staring at her in complete bewilderment.

"I'm—I'm terribly sorry," choked out the girl. "Please let me ride just a few blocks until I can think what to do. Please don't stop where he can get me."

She was addressing both the driver and his passenger impartially, and the driver tossed back over his shoulder curtly, "It's all right with me, lady, long as my fare don't mind. That your old man chasing you back there?"

They were two blocks from the hotel now, and he rounded a corner, letting the motor idle down while he half-turned his head interestedly.

His original passenger said quietly, "It's all right, of course, driver." She had a young and throaty voice, and spoke as calmly as though it were the most ordinary thing in the world for her to share her taxi with strangers who came running desperately out of dark alleys practically gibbering with fright.

"Oh, no," said the girl, still gasping for breath and jerking out the words between gasps. "Not my husband. He's—I don't *know*," she cried out tearfully. "I can't *think*. It's all so unreal—so horrible."

"Well, look here, Miss. You want I should find us a cop and report it? They'll pick him up quick."

"Oh, no! I don't think so. Not the police. They're—they won't believe me. They just won't. They'll ask all sorts of questions—" Her voice trailed off miserably.

"What do you wanta do?" asked the driver patiently. "I got this other fare, see? She's paying her money—"

"It's perfectly all right, driver," the placid young voice said again from the right corner of the rear seat. They were approaching Biscayne Boulevard now, and she suggested, "Just turn toward Flagler, why don't you, and I'll tell you where to drop me."

"I don't know what I should do," sighed the other girl forlornly. "That horrible man—" She lapsed into silence for a moment, then seemed to realize she owed her benefactors some sort explanation for the scene they had witnessed.

"If I go to the police, they'll say I'm crazy. I'm not, but I can't prove it."

"I betcha can't, sister," muttered the driver under his breath as he swung left onto the Boulevard.

"But somebody's got to help me," she went on desperately. "My brother—" She sucked in her breath, then exhaled it slowly and went on more calmly. "I'm a stranger in Miami. Perhaps you'd know, driver. Some private detective. An honest one. Who'd listen to me and not think I'm crazy, and help me."

"You might try Mike Shayne, Miss. He always seems to be getting himself mixed up in screwy cases."

"Is he—a good detective?"

"Best in Miami. Best in the country, I guess," added the driver with civic pride. "You need somebody to handle that gink was chasing you with no questions asked, Shayne's your man."

"It isn't exactly that. It's—but I can't waste time talking about it," burst out the girl distractedly. "Would there be any chance of contacting him at night like this?"

"Lady," said the driver, "you picked out just the right cab when you jumped in front of me back there and like to got yourself killed. I always read the write-ups on Shayne's cases in the papers and I know exactly where he hangs out at night. And from what I read in the papers, I guess he does as much work at home at night as he does in his office." There was the faintest suggestion of a leer in the driver's voice, but the girl disregarded it.

She said eagerly, "Could you take me there?" Her fingers nervously clutched a black suede handbag in her lap. "I can pay you—I'll be glad to pay."

The driver said, "It's only a few blocks on ahead now. If the other lady don't really mind—?"

"Go right ahead, driver." A crisply amused voice came from the girl's companion. "I honestly haven't decided yet where I want you to drop me."

"Okay then." The driver passed brightly-lighted Flagler Street and turned right at the next corner. A few moments later he drew up in front of an apartment hotel on the north bank of the Miami River and reached back to unlatch the left door. "You go right in here, Miss, and ask at the desk for Michael Shayne. Nobody's going to bother you any in here."

Starting to get out, the girl drew in a deep breath and told her companion, "I can't thank you enough. I—I just can't explain, but you've been wonderful to let me share your cab. I'll give the driver enough to cover wherever you want to go."

"That's not necessary. It's been a real pleasure—and very exciting."

As the girl slid out in front of the hotel, she pressed a five-dollar bill into the driver's hand. She breathed, "You've been wonderful."

He looked at the bill and pushed his peaked cap back to scratch his forehead as he watched the girl hurry inside the lobby. "Screwy dames," he muttered. "It sure takes all kinds—" Then he shrugged and settled his cap down firmly, turned to ask formally, "Where to now, Miss?"

THREE: *9:39 P.M.*

The running man slid angrily to a panting stop half a block north of the Hibiscus Hotel as the taxi ahead of him gathered speed and the red taillights grew dimmer and then disappeared around a corner.

He gritted his teeth together hard and slammed one fist into an open palm in a gesture of frustrated anger. In the light from the street lamp at the corner ahead where the taxi had stopped to pick up its passenger, he had seen the name of the taxi company and the car's license number.

He hesitated only a moment, then turned and strode back to the hotel behind him. Entering the lobby, empty except for the desk clerk and switchboard operator whispering together excitedly, he glanced around and went directly to a telephone booth near the door with a local directory on the shelf outside.

He looked up the street address of the taxi company he sought, made a notation of it and went out to a car parked at the curb just south of the entrance. He got in and drove to the address he had written down, on Northwest 8th Avenue, and found it to be a large garage with taxis filling all the parking spaces in front.

He parked up the street and returned, found a large, lighted office on the ground level with drivers lounging about in front, half a dozen others seated in chairs against the wall inside.

Beyond, there was a large desk with a burly, red-faced man seated behind it talking into a telephone. Beyond him, in a cubby-hole, a thin, faded blonde was talking in

a bored voice into a microphone suspended from the wall
in front of her.

The lounging drivers looked at him curiously as he entered and went directly to the desk. The burly man put
down the phone and called back over his shoulder, "Number two-oh-three, Gert. Pickup at one-forty-seven Brickell,"
and looked up to ask, "Want a taxi, Mister?"

"Not exactly." The tall man with the scarred face
frowned and leaned forward with his palms flat on the
desk. "How much chance is there to get in touch with the
driver of one of your cabs—if I can give you his license
number?"

"Not much. If you've got his name or the number of his
hack—"

His telephone burred. He scooped it up and said, "Yeh?"
listened a moment and said, "Right away," looked over at
one of the seated drivers and said, "You better take it, Tom.
The Starbright Club. He sounded tight enough for a good
tip."

In the meantime the man in front of the desk had gotten
out his wallet. He drew out a ten, hesitated, and added
another ten to it on the desk. He said, "You must have
records showing the license number of each cab."

"Sure we got records," grunted the burly man. "But
hell! It's late and there's only a skeleton staff in the office."
He jerked his head to the left where an open door showed
two girls working at desks inside.

The man said, "It's really very important. Matter of life
and death, you might say, for me to find about a fare this
cab picked up near the Hibiscus Hotel about twenty minutes ago." He reached for a piece of paper and wrote down
the license number he had memorized.

The man at the desk shrugged and said, "That makes
it easier. Hibiscus, twenty minutes ago." He pushed back
his chair and went back to confer with the blonde radio
dispatcher, and they consulted a chart together and he

made some notations on the paper with the license number.

Then he went into the other room and gave the paper to one of the girls with brief instructions, and returned to his desk, grunting, "Should have it in a few minutes."

His phone continued to ring at intervals, while the man stood stiffly in front of the desk, waiting.

It was almost ten minutes before the girl came in and put the paper in front of him. He glanced at it and said affably, "That's Archie. Number sixty-two. That what you wanted?" His thick fingers gathered up the two ten-dollar bills.

"I want you to get him over his radio. Find out where he took the woman he picked up in the street near the Hibiscus half an hour ago."

Blunt fingertips drummed thoughtfully on the desk. "That ain't regular, Mister. You want to wait around till Archie checks in. Then if he wants to bother going back over his trip schedule for you—"

"I need it now—fast," the man said impatiently. "It's my sister, see? And she's in bad trouble. I've got to find her in a hurry. Isn't twenty enough for a small favor like that?"

The big man shrugged. He put the twenty in his pocket and said coldly, "You paid that for Archie's name and cab number." He held out the slip and gestured toward a gate in the low railing beside his desk. "Go back and talk to Gertie if you want. None of my business what she puts over the mike."

The man with the scarred face compressed his lips, picked up the paper and strode back to stand beside the dispatcher. She completed a message, pressed a button and looked up at him appraisingly.

He asked, "Can you call Archie in number sixty-two on that thing?"

She said, "That's what it's for."

"Will you do it and ask him where he took the young

lady he picked up in the street a block from the Hibiscus
Hotel about half an hour ago?"

"Gee, Mister. I dunno. We're not supposed to send any
personal messages over the radio. That's company regula-
tions."

"But this is very important. I've got to locate my sister.
She's—" He drew in a deep breath and went on, "Well,
she's in real bad trouble. Danger, maybe. Might save her
life if I get to her fast."

The blonde screwed her face up in a troubled manner
and turned to call past him to the man at the desk. "What
you think, Bert?"

He shrugged without turning his head. "You're on your
own, kid. I never know what you say over that mike."

The man was getting his wallet out again. The dispatcher watched him covertly as he reluctantly withdrew
another ten.

Then she punched a button and droned, "Calling car
sixty-two. Sixty-two. Come in, Archie." She pressed another button and leaned back with her head-phones to
wait.

After thirty seconds, she said, "Archie. There's a man
here wants to know where you took a lady fare you picked
up a block from the Hibiscus half an hour ago."

She listened and then asked her questioner: "Which way
from the Hibiscus? North or south?"

He thought quickly, closing his eyes to remember and
orient himself. "Tell him north. Just the first block north."

She told Archie that. Then her eyes rounded and she
turned to say, "Archie wants to know if you're the guy that
was chasing her. That she was so scared of."

"Good God, no," he exclaimed impatiently. "I tell you
she's my sister. That man chasing her—he's the one I'm
afraid of. Tell the driver she's in danger and I must get to
her before it's too late."

She gave Archie this answer over the microphone and

listened again. Then she reached out and tweaked the ten-dollar bill from his hand and told him:

"Archie says he guesses it don't matter much either way whether you are the guy or not. Because he took her to see Michael Shayne, and if you feel like tangling with that redhead, he'd like to be around to see it."

"Michael Shayne? Who's he?"

"You *must* be a stranger here, Mister. He's that private eye that's always getting write-ups in the papers."

"A private detective?" The man bit his underlip nerv-ously, then said, "Well, she's probably safe enough then, but I'd still like to see her. Did this Archie say where Shayne is?"

"Yeh." She gave him the address of the hotel Archie had relayed to her. He muttered, "Thanks—a lot," and ran out of the office to his car.

FOUR: *9:48 P.M.*

There was a faint moon overhead and the night air of early autumn had a sensuously somnolent feel about it. There was a strongly lingering warmth from the earth after the heat of the day's sun, rising to mingle languidly with a faint inshore breeze from the Atlantic.

Driving southward at a moderate pace on the right-hand lane of Biscayne Boulevard as it entered the city, Michael Shayne glanced sideways and downward, approvingly, at the brown head of Lucy Hamilton pressed lightly against the shoulder of his white linen jacket.

He was bare-headed, and his coarse red hair was ruffled pleasantly by the night breeze. His big hands were loosely on the wheel and a feeling of contentment and relaxation gripped him.

This was the really good time of the year in Miami, he reflected. The worst heat of the summer had passed, yet the vanguard of sun-seekers from the North had not yet arrived to take over the Magic City. He hadn't a single case in his files, and probably wouldn't have for a month or more—until the quick-money boys and the suckers arrived in droves and his particular talents would become much in demand.

Lucy rubbed her cheek unashamedly against his right bicep, and said in a muffled voice, "Wake me when we get home, Michael. I'm afraid that last glass of champagne knocked me for a loop."

He chuckled indulgently. "I like you when you're looped, angel."

"What a horrible thing to say." She lifted her head momentarily in order to be properly indignant, and then snuggled it back again.

"Not at all," he protested cheerfully. "You sort of take your hair down and forget about being the prim and proper secretary."

"As if I were ever that," she scoffed.

"Of course you are. You never make a semblance of a pass at me during office hours. I have to take you out, buy you an expensive dinner and ply you with Pol Roger before you act properly human."

"Pol Roger? You know darned well that champagne came from California."

"Anyhow, it looped you. And we'll be home pretty soon and I'm going to take advantage of your condition and kiss you."

"Why?"

"Why what?"

"Why bother?" Her voice remained muffled and sleepy, but an underlying note of intensity crept into it.

"Why bother kissing you?" he asked in perplexity.

"Exactly."

He drove on down the Boulevard, maintaining the same steady, relaxed pace, as he pondered her question and his reply. Basically, he knew what she meant. And it was difficult to find an intelligent answer to her question. Because he liked kissing her, of course. But that wasn't enough. Not enough to really answer the question she had posed.

What she was really asking was—where did it get them?

And the only honest answer to that was—nowhere, really. She didn't ask that sort of question often. Mostly, she seemed perfectly content with "things as they were." To drift along through the days as a cheerful and most efficient secretary in his office—to accept without question as many evenings like this as he could contrive for her (or wanted to contrive for her).

He stirred uneasily and lifted one hand in an unconscious gesture to tug at the lobe of his ear. Very quietly, he asked, "Would you change things if you could, Lucy?"

She sat up then, and moved slightly away from him as though this tack in the discussion required a little more formality between them. "I don't know." Her voice was grave and honestly dubious. "I just don't know, Michael."

They were below 79th Street now, rapidly approaching the side street that led to her apartment.

He turned his head briefly to study her profile in the street lights, and she met his gaze intently. For a moment there was a queer sense of strain between them. He broke it by turning his attention back to driving and saying lightly:

"Maybe time has caught up with us, angel. I feel this is a matter for serious discussion over a drink. Any cognac at your place?"

"You know there is. Whatever was left in the bottle the last time you were there."

"I never feel sure. Can't get it out of my thick head that one of these days you'll start feeding some other guy the stuff."

"Maybe I will. One of these days."

He slowed, approaching her corner, slanting over into the left-hand lane, gauging approaching traffic to cut through it without coming to a full stop.

Neither of them said anything more until he drew up to the curb in front of her apartment building and got out. He went around to open the door for her, took her elbow to help her out, then put his other hand under her other elbow and held her a moment looking down into her lightly flushed face. She made no move to push closer or to draw back. She stood quiescent, waiting.

His fingers tightened on the soft flesh of her arms and his voice was unaccountably husky as he said, "Lucy?"

She said, "Yes, Michael?"

He bent to brush his lips across her forehead just below the tendrils of brown hair, then turned to tuck her arm into his and led her toward the entrance.

There was a small foyer, and Lucy unlocked the inner door with a key from her purse. He held the door for her to precede him inside and up the single flight of stairs. Following her closely, Michael Shayne's red head remained level with her slender waist.

There is something peculiarly intimate, he thought fleetingly, about a man following a woman up a flight of stairs. Something almost decisive about it. As though, somehow, a die had been irrevocably cast. It was a crazy thought and he tried to brush it aside. He had often followed Lucy up these same stairs for a night-cap after spending a pleasant evening together. But unaccountably it was different tonight, and he felt a surge of gladness within him that it was different.

She turned aside at the first landing to unlock her apartment door. He waited silently until she turned on the light, and then followed her inside. She wore a semi-evening gown of very dark blue silk that had a sort of glitter to it. It was perfectly simple, cut low in front and back and with narrow straps over the shoulders that left a good portion of creamy flesh bare.

He watched her speculatively as she crossed the long pleasant room toward the kitchenette, saying over her shoulder with a faint smile, "Make yourself comfortable while I get out the makings."

It was easy to make oneself comfortable here, he conceded as he dropped into a deep chair beside the sofa and lit a cigarette. The room was uncluttered, but nicely and intelligently furnished.

He stretched his long legs in front of him, leaned his head back and closed his eyes and let smoke come out through both nostrils.

All right. Why didn't he marry Lucy? Tonight, he decided grimly, he was going to face the question squarely. He was going to ask her to face it squarely with him. Something neither of them had done before, though they had been on the verge of it many times.

He straightened up in the chair as he heard the swish of her full skirt re-entering the room. She carried a tray with a squat bottle of cognac, a four-ounce wine glass, a tumbler with ice cubes in it for herself, another tumbler filled with ice and water for him to sip while he drank cognac from the wine glass.

She set the tray down on a low table in front of the sofa, seated herself in the corner close to Shayne's chair, and filled the four-ounce glass with cognac. Then she poured an inch in the bottom of her tumbler, and held his glass out to him.

Her telephone rang before he could take the glass.

An extraordinary change came over Lucy's face. The shrill, insistent ring of the phone shattered her placidity as the glassy surface of a still pond is shattered by a stone tossed into the center.

She continued to hold the glass out for him, and said hotly, "I shan't answer it. It'll be for you, of course. No one would be calling me at this hour."

"All the more reason for you to answer it," said Shayne. "It might be important."

"A blonde?" she asked tautly.

He said easily, "Or a brunette." The telephone kept on ringing. With a gesture of impatience, he rose and crossed to it in two strides. He swept it up with his back to her and said, "Miss Hamilton's apartment," into the mouthpiece. Then he said, "That's right," and listened, his right hand going up to rub his jaw absently.

Watching him, Lucy Hamilton compressed her lips tightly and set his untouched glass of cognac back on the tray. It was a limp gesture of surrender.

With his back to her, he said incisively, "All right, Pete. I'll be there in five minutes."

He replaced the phone and turned, shaking his head sadly though his gray eyes were alert and not at all unhappy.

"Sorry as the devil, angel. But that was—"

"A blonde," she supplied for him. "A blonde in distress, no less. Just dying to weep on Mike Shayne's broad shoulder."

"Pete didn't say," he returned absently, looking around for his hat and then remembering he hadn't worn one. He suddenly became conscious of the bitterness in her face, and stepped contritely forward to touch her cheek with his fingertips. "This really sounds important. You know I've told the hotel never to bother calling me here unless it was."

"I know," she said dully, looking down so her eyes would not meet his. "So why don't you get on your white charger and ride? What's keeping you?"

"You know I'm sorry," Shayne said again. His jaw tightened when she still refused to look up. He turned to the door, saying calmly, "Keep that drink for me. I'll be back before midnight."

FIVE: *10:00 P.M.*

The lobby of Shayne's hotel was deserted except for the night clerk behind the desk and one young woman nervously smoking a cigarette in an over-stuffed chair on one side facing the doorway as Shayne entered.

He glanced at the woman briefly as he went to the desk. She appeared quite young and pretty, wore a dark skirt, a white blouse with a light gray jacket over it, and had a red patent-leather handbag in her lap. Her eyes followed him as he strode to the desk where Pete leaned forward eagerly, his thin face screwed up in a grimace, pale eyebrows moving up and down with excitement.

"I didn't know whether to call you at Miss Hamilton's or not, Mr. Shayne." He kept his voice furtively low, as though he feared being overheard. "But you did give me that number once, for me to try if I thought it was important, and this time I decided it was. She *said* it was, see? And acted scared to death. You know, looking back over her shoulder like she thought she was maybe being tailed—like the devil himself might be after her. And you told me once before it was all right to send somebody up to your room to wait for you to come back, and so I thought—"

"If she were pretty enough," Shayne reminded him with a grin. "Is she?"

"Yeh. Real pretty." Pete's answering grin was relieved by Shayne's evidence of good humor, and it took on a sly man-to-man quality. "Not, that is to say, for my money, anything like as hot a piece as this here other one sitting yonder." He jerked his thumb toward the girl with the red pocketbook. "But then she didn't come in till later, see, so I couldn't very easy send her up, too. Could I?" he asked anxiously.

Shayne rested one elbow on the counter and pivoted to look at the girl across the lobby. Watching them closely, it must have been evident to her that she was under discussion, for she promptly got up and hurried toward them.

She was extremely well filled-out for her age, which didn't appear to be more than twenty, and her hips twitched provocatively as she approached. Her eyes were very light blue and had a peculiar glassy quality, lashes and brows so thin and light as to seem almost non-existent. She had too much lipstick on a very full and pouting mouth which she spread in a hopeful smile as she came up fast, asking, "Are you Mr. Shayne?"

Shayne nodded without speaking, studying her through narrowed eyes as she looked past him at Pete and demanded viciously, "Well, why didn't you say so? You promised me as soon as he came in—"

"And I just came in," said Shayne quietly. "I'm afraid I haven't time for—"

"You've got time for me." Her fingers caught his arm and tugged at it, pulling him away from the desk toward a corner where they would be out of ear-shot. "It's terribly important," she hurried on in a too-consciously throaty voice for one so young. "I've been waiting and waiting and just about going crazy wondering what I'd do if you didn't get back in time. But it's all right because I know he'll still be there if you go right away. He was there fifteen minutes ago. The Silver Glade. It's right down the street."

She had her leather bag open as she spoke, and was digging into it. Her hand came out with a four-by-six photograph of a young man which she thrust into Shayne's hand.

"That's him. Please hurry so you'll be waiting outside

when he comes out. Then follow him wherever he goes."

Shayne shook his red head bluntly. "Sorry, but I'm already working. And if it's a divorce job—"

"What does it matter to you what sort of job it is? I can pay you. How much? Please. It probably won't be more than half an hour." She was digging in her bag again, and came out with a roll of bills. She began to peel twenties off it, pausing on the fifth to look at Shayne hopefully, then detaching two more as he kept on shaking his head stubbornly.

He held the photograph out for her to take back, but she pushed it away, saying fiercely, "You can't refuse. He'll be gone before I can get anyone else." Her voice became tremulous with supplication, and she pressed herself close to him, looking up into his eyes beseechingly and pouting her too-red lips invitingly.

"Pretty please." She tried to force the seven bills into his hand. "I'll be waiting for you to report. At my place. Alone." She cooed the last four words throatily, giving them a thoroughly seductive connotation.

He said, "No," shortly, wishing she were old enough to realize her too-blatant perfume wasn't at all as seductive as she probably imagined it to be. He pushed the man's photograph back into her hand and turned away impatiently, but she clung to him and tried to pull him back, sliding the photo into his jacket pocket and continuing to try and force the bills into his hand.

He kept on toward the desk, thrusting her aside impatiently, and she finally gave up and stood still, staring at him with both hands on her ample hips, her pale blue eyes glittering with fury.

Shayne didn't look back at her, and Pete was grinning widely. "Sure got 'em fighting over you tonight, Mr. Shayne. Now if that there one was to push up to me like that—"

"Is the one up in my room anything like her?" Shayne

interrupted impatiently.

"Not a bit of it. Well, she's pretty all right, but you couldn't tell much about her, she was so scared." He lowered his voice and looked past Shayne. "This'n came in a few minutes ago, and *she* wanted to go up to your room to wait for you. But I wouldn't tell her the number no matter what kind of eye she gave me. Didn't tell her you already had one client waiting up there."

"Fine," said Shayne impatiently. "Don't give her my number." He turned to the elevator where there was a car waiting, and lengthened his stride when he saw her start moving toward him again.

Her running heels clacked loudly behind him as he strode in past the grinning operator and snapped, "Shut the door fast."

The operator got it shut before she reached the car. Shayne mopped sweat from his forehead with his sleeve and answered the operator's grin with one of his own. He said, "Up, Jack. And no matter what methods of persuasion that doll tries to use, don't bring her up to my floor. You got that?"

"You bet, Mr. Shayne. Might be fun at that—her trying to persuade a guy."

Shayne grunted noncommittally and got off to go down the corridor to his suite.

SIX: *10:06 P.M.*

Shayne's first impression of the girl who cowered away from him at the other end of his sitting room was that she was quite young and pretty, a honey-blonde, and practically frightened to death by his abrupt entrance.

Her face was dead white, her eyes as round as two marbles, her mouth slack and quivering as she shrank back against the wall staring at him.

She straightened herself, still tremulous as he closed the door firmly behind him, and asked quaveringly, "Are you Mr. Shayne?"

"Of course I'm Shayne," he said irritably. "You came here asking for me, didn't you? This is my room. Who did you think would be coming in?"

"I didn't know. I've been so horribly frightened waiting. I thought *he* might have followed me here somehow."

Shayne said, "He?" She still stood flat against the wall as though she were afraid she couldn't stand up without some support, and her whole body trembled as though gripped by an uncontrollable ague. He moved toward her slowly, with a feeling that any sudden movement on his part might frighten her into complete hysteria.

"The man who—killed my brother," she gasped out. "That is, I guess he did. I know he must have. If—if my brother is really dead. But he *is*. He must be. I saw him, I tell you. You'll believe me, won't you, Mr. Shayne? You won't think I'm crazy when I tell you?"

Shayne was close to her now. Close enough to stretch out a long arm and take hold of one of her wrists and pull her gently away from the wall. He held her wrist very tightly as he guided her to a deep chair and pressed her down into it. He made his voice calm and soothing as he said, "Of course I'll listen to you. Just take it easy now. What you need is a drink first. Close your eyes and relax. Stop worrying about anyone getting to you in here."

He let go her wrist and turned to the wall liquor cabinet near the kitchen. "Brandy or sherry?"

"A little sherry, please." Her voice had lost its hysterical shrillness, was low and faltering. "You've just got to believe me."

Shayne didn't reply. He got down a bottle of cocktail sherry and one of cognac, went into the small kitchen and reappeared a few minutes later with a tray holding wine glasses and a tumbler of ice water. He moved a small table close to the girl's chair, put the tray on it and poured her a glass of sherry.

"Drink that first—all of it—before you say anything else." He filled his own glass with cognac and took a pleased sip of it, regretfully remembering the untouched glass he'd left in Lucy's apartment just to come over here and listen to some sort of loony story about a hysterical girl's brother who must be dead but maybe wasn't after all. He pulled another chair around so that it faced her, sat in it and waited patiently until she had completely emptied her sherry glass.

"Now," he said. "Tell me about your brother. You say he's been murdered?"

"Yes. I tell you I saw him. Lying there dead, right in front of my eyes. But he *wasn't* there when I came back. He was gone. Just vanished." She shuddered violently and flung out both hands. "But he couldn't be. Dead men can't just get up and walk away, can they?"

"None of them I've met," Shayne agreed absently. "You'd better start at the beginning and give me all of it."

"Yes. Of course." She nodded vehemently and brightly,

as though she thought Shayne was just wonderful to have thought of that.

"It began tonight, really. Well, 'way back before to-night, I guess you could say. With my brother being weak and foolish about girls, I mean. And I've always sort of looked after him. Ever since father died four years ago. He's two years older than I am, actually, but, well—he always needed looking after, sort of."

She paused, biting her underlip fiercely, her light brown eyes looking past Shayne as though they gazed at some-thing far-away or long-ago.

"Let's get back to tonight," suggested Shayne.

"Of course." She gave her head a little jerk and smiled timidly. "Well, we're at the Roney Plaza. For the past two weeks. And I've been seeing the signs. I *knew* he had some girl on the string and I'd have to be taking a hand soon, but— Well, tonight, about nine o'clock he called me and he was terribly worried and frightened. He said I had to come over right away. To the Hibiscus Hotel here in Miami. To room three-sixteen. I made him repeat it and I wrote it down so there wouldn't be any mistake. So I got a taxi to the Hibiscus at once." She paused to swallow hard, and Shayne leaned forward to pour more sherry in her glass. She appeared not to notice him.

"So I went right up to the third floor," she continued in a strained voice, "and to room three-sixteen. Light came through the transom, but no one answered when I knocked on the door. I—I knocked three times and called out his name, and then I tried the knob. It wasn't locked. It opened right up. And the first thing I saw was my brother lying on the bed right across the room. He was in his shirt sleeves and his coat was rolled up under his head and there was b-blood. There was a big jagged hole in his throat. I—I knew he was dead. He *had* to be, Mr. Shayne. His eyes were open and glazed." She put her face down suddenly into her hands and began sobbing.

Shayne let her cry it out. He lighted a cigarette and drank half his cognac and took a sip of ice water, and her shoulders began to stop shaking.

He said quietly, "The sooner you get on with it, the sooner I may be able to do something."

"I know. Of course." She lifted a tear-wet face and swallowed hard. "I didn't even go into the room. I didn't have to. I *knew* he was dead. I thought of using the phone in the room, but then thought of spoiling fingerprints on it— if they might be clues, you know, and I remembered that when I got off the elevator I'd noticed a door to a lighted room standing open. So I flew down there to ask them to report it, and the door was still open but no one was inside. So I grabbed up that phone and called down to the switchboard and told them. Then I went back. I couldn't have been gone more than two minutes. I *know* I couldn't. But the door to three-sixteen was shut when I got there— and I know I'd left it open. But the light was still on, and when I tried the knob it opened just as it had before. *But he wasn't there any more.* He just wasn't. And there was no sign of anything wrong. No coat. No blood. Nothing."

"Sure it was the right room?"

"Of course I'm sure. I'd checked the number as soon as I found the door closed. So I ran inside and looked in the bathroom and the only closet and I even peeked under the bed. I felt as though I'd gone through the looking glass. Like Alice, you know. And I ran out into the hall and he jumped at me." She stopped, her mouth open and breathing hard as she relived the horror of the moment.

"Some man I didn't recognize," she went on more slowly. "I'm sure I never saw him before. The light in the hallway was dim, but I got one look at his face as he jumped at me. A horrible, scarred face. I whirled around and ran in the opposite direction toward a red signal light showing the stairway and he shouted something I couldn't understand and ran after me.

"I never looked back once. I knew he must have murdered my brother and I'd be next. I tore through the door and down three flights of stairs and there was an open door at the back leading out to a narrow pitch-dark alley. I ran as fast as I could toward the lighted street with him behind me shouting for me to stop. And just as I got to the street a taxicab came along and I jumped in front of it and made the driver stop. Then I tumbled in and shouted for him to drive away fast and he did. And then— and then I didn't know what to do and the driver was awfully nice and when I told him sort of—a little bit of what had happened—he mentioned you and said you could help me if anyone in Miami could and he brought me here."

"Nice of him to recommend me," grunted Shayne. "But why not the police? They're the ones you're supposed to report dead bodies to."

"I was afraid to go to them." She shuddered violently and reached for her sherry glass. "I've always heard they're inefficient and corrupt, and I knew they'd laugh at me and say I was crazy. Besides, I knew the hotel would have reported my call to them, and after they'd gone up and then not found any body there after all, they certainly wouldn't listen to me."

Shayne shrugged. He got up, saying, "Take another sip of that sherry while I check."

He crossed to the center table, gave a number, and a moment later, said, "Sergeant Jenkins, please. Hi, Sarge. Mike Shayne. You had any report of trouble at the Hibiscus Hotel? Any sort of trouble. Murders or any little thing like that?" He listened a moment, then said slowly, "I see. No, I guess not. Not just yet. If anything does pop, I'll let you know."

He hung up, looking across at the back of the girl's blonde head gleaming in the overhead light, massaging his ear-lobe gently. She turned to look at him with a hopeful expression which died away when he shook his head. He thumbed through the directory for the Hibiscus, called it and asked to be connected with Mr. Patton.

Then he said, "Ollie? Mike Shayne. Any excitement at your place around nine-thirty?"

He listened for quite a time while the girl continued to sit twisted in her chair so she could watch his face. Finally he said, "Thanks, Ollie. Any time I can give you a hand—" He hung up and returned to his chair with a scowl.

"The house detective at the Hibiscus gives it about the way you tell it. The first part, that is. They don't know anything about you being chased out of the hotel. They had the call you say you made from three-sixty about a murdered man and went there first because the switchboard girl thought you must mean that room instead of three-sixteen which she first thought you said. But they checked both rooms carefully and found no body nor any trace of murder. So they didn't report it to the police, naturally. Thinking it was a hoax—or the work of some nutty female." He studied the girl's face carefully as he spoke, and she noted his expression and cried out despairingly:

"You think so too, don't you? That I'm crazy? That I'm just making it all up?"

He shrugged noncommittally. "Not necessarily. The man chasing you through the alley sounds real enough. Did the taxi driver happen to see him too?" he added casually.

"Yes, he did. And also the lady who was in the cab when I hailed it. You can ask them both."

"Get the number of the cab or the driver's name?"

"N-no."

"Or the name of the other passenger?"

"No. Oh, you're just as bad as I knew the police would be," she flared out, getting to her feet abruptly and swaying a little. "How can I *prove* it? But I know my brother's been murdered. I saw him. It wasn't any hallucination."

"Sit back down," Shayne said soothingly. "I'm sure you saw something to make you believe that. I'm not denying anything. Let's see if we can figure it out. Is your brother any sort of practical joker?"

"No." She reseated herself stiffly.

"Because," Shayne said, "there is an old gag that's been pulled off with a bottle of ketchup."

"After the victim's throat has been cut?" she demanded angrily. "Mr. Shayne, I saw the gaping hole. And his *eyes*. Staring and—dead."

Shayne got up and began to stride back and forth across the room. "You didn't go in the first time. Didn't make even a cursory search?"

"No. My only thought was to get to a telephone."

"So the murderer could have been in there—in the bathroom or closet?"

"I suppose so. I didn't look."

"And how long would you say you were gone to find another phone?"

"Not more than two minutes, I think. Three or four at the very most. I didn't waste any time going or coming."

Shayne shrugged and said doubtfully, "If it weren't for the man chasing you, I'd have to think you had some sort of hallucination about seeing your brother. As it is— I still don't see what I can do, but I will go over to the Hibiscus with you and get hold of the house detective and check the whole thing a little more thoroughly than they probably did the first time."

The idea of returning to the Hibiscus appeared to frighten her all over again, and she asked despairingly, "Do I have to? Go there with you? Can't I just be your client, and you do the checking?" Her hands eagerly opened the black suede bag in her lap. "I've got money here. Plenty of cash. I can pay you a retainer."

Shayne shook his head, studying her harassed features

very carefully. "Right now I'm not at all sure there's any case for me to take a retainer on." He didn't tell her the truth—that he didn't like crazy clients and that he was beginning to suspect she was as nutty as a fruit-cake.

But the look of utter desperation that settled over her at his words moved him to go on hastily, "Suppose I nose around and see what I can find out. If anything has happened to your brother, it'll be time enough to talk about a retainer." He stood up briskly. "I suppose I can reach you at the Roney? What's your name and room number?"

"Do I have to go back there?" She shuddered and her eyes were liquidly appealing. "Whoever did that to my brother must know where we're staying. I keep seeing that awful, scarred face in my mind. I—I—couldn't I just stay here while you go and see?"

Shayne hesitated, his angular face tightening. God only knew what sort of tensions were working on her. Without pretending to be any sort of psychologist, here was a persecution complex, if he'd ever encountered one. First, she had been afraid to go to the police with her story. Now, she was afraid to go back to the safety of her own hotel room. Definitely, he didn't want her hanging around his place alone, prey to all sorts of unreasoning fears.

Not unkindly, he said, "I don't think that would be such a good idea, but I've got a much better one." He crossed to the center table and opened a drawer to take out a sheet of his office paper. With a pen he wrote Lucy Hamilton's name and address on it, and added a brief note:

> Angel:
> Be just that and take care of the bearer. Put your chain on the door and don't let *anyone* in to her until you hear from me. She may be in great danger.

He signed the note "Mike," and handed it to her to read. "My secretary," he explained. "We'll go down and

I'll put you in a taxi for her place. No one can possibly find you there, and I'll know exactly where you are when I need you."

Her eyes shone mistily with gratitude as she read it. Her voice quavered. "You're—just wonderful. I could kiss that taxi driver for bringing me to you."

Shayne turned away from her before her gratitude spilled over into kissing him instead, because that was what her look portended. And he liked to be fairly certain the women he kissed were sane.

At that moment there was the sound of loud footsteps in the hall outside. They stopped at his door and there was an authoritative knock.

She shuddered and cringed away from the door, staring at it with round, mesmerized eyes, as though she expected it to come crashing inward momentarily.

"It must be he! I knew he'd follow me here. Don't let him in. Please don't let him in."

Shayne said, "For God's sake," impatiently and started toward the door. She grabbed him and tried to hold him back as there was another knock and a harsh voice demanding, "Open up, Shayne."

"Please," she cried piteously, clinging to him. "I'll die if you let him in. Isn't there any place I can go?"

Shayne looked down at her curiously. Her face had gone all to pieces with terror. She clung to him limply as a rag doll.

He said harshly, "Snap out of it. No one's going to bother you while I'm here."

He could just as well have slapped her. She cringed away from the impact of his voice like a cur that has just been kicked resoundingly. Her mouth worked soundlessly and there were bubbles of spittle on her lips.

Shayne put his hands on her shoulders and turned her about. "Go in the kitchen. There's a latch on the inside. Lock it and stay there until I call for you to come out." He gave her a gentle shove, stood there and watched her scurry back to the kitchen and close the door.

The knocking and demands for entrance continued at the front door, and he turned and stalked to it grimly, jerked it open to confront a tall young man with a scarred face who stood on the threshold.

SEVEN: *10:20 P.M.*

The scarred face, almost level with Shayne's, was red and contorted with anger or some other emotion, but it was not fearsome or hideous as the girl's description had led Shayne to expect. Indeed, discounting the scar on one cheek and the evidence of undue emotion, Shayne perceived it would have been a pleasant, almost handsome face of a well set-up man in his early thirties.

The scar ran diagonally from the left corner of his mouth upward to the point of a rather high cheek-bone, and Shayne guessed that normally it would not draw too much attention. But now it was a white weal against the suffused flesh and stood out clearly.

Shayne stood flat-footed and immobile in the doorway, glowering at his visitor who moved to push forward, demanding furiously, "Where is she? What's happened to Nellie?"

Shayne put a big hand against the younger man's chest and pushed him backward. He growled. "You haven't been invited in. What the hell do you mean by this ruckus?"

"You're Shayne, aren't you?" The young man glared back at him defiantly and his hands balled into fists. "I'm coming in whether I'm invited or not, and no two-bit private dick is going to keep me out."

Shayne studied him speculatively, his gray eyes bleak and trenches deepening in his cheeks. He said, "Whenever you're ready to try your luck, bud."

For a long moment their eyes locked and held. The younger man's blood-shot and humid, Shayne's coldly

challenging. Then with a supreme effort of will, his visitor
forced his body to relax. He unballed his fists and blinked
a couple of times, wet dry lips with his tongue. He said
hoarsely, "I'm sorry I tried to barge in. I'm Bert Paulson
and I'm so goddamned worried about Nellie I'm just about
off my rocker."

"So, that makes two of you," Shayne thought to himself. Aloud, he said, "That's better. Keep it that way and
maybe we'll get along." He swung abruptly on his heel to
let Paulson enter, walked back to the tray holding his
cognac glass still half-full. He made no attempt to conceal
the bottle of sherry and the glass the girl had used. He
took a sip of cognac and turned to see Paulson striding
belligerently in, looking suspiciously all about the room
and at the three closed doors leading to bathroom, bedroom and kitchen.

"So her name is Nellie?" said Shayne pleasantly. "Funny,
but I just now realized she didn't tell me."

"Where is she? What's happened to her, Shayne? What
in the name of God made her act that way when she saw
me?"

"What way? Have a drink, Paulson?" Shayne waved his
hand toward the open liquor cabinet.

"No, thanks. Didn't she tell you? What kind of crazy
story did she cook up to explain why she came here?"

"She told me several things." Shayne dropped into a
chair with his glass. "I assure you she's perfectly okay and
I will produce her whenever you convince me it's safe to
do so."

"Safe?" snorted Paulson angrily. "Why in the name of
God is she afraid of *me*?"

"Suppose you sit down and tell me."

With another lingering look at the three closed doors
leading off the sitting room, Paulson sat stiffly on the edge
of the chair in front of the redhead.

"*I* don't know. Unless she's really slipped a cog this

time." Paulson's eyes burned into Shayne's. "How did she act? Is she completely insane?" His voice was strained and hoarse and he thudded his right fist into his palm. "Damn it, man! Don't you see—"

"I don't see very much right now," Shayne interrupted him. "So far as I could tell she made at least as much sense as you do right now. Calm down and try to give me a coherent story."

"Did she tell you about screaming and running from me in the hotel the moment she saw my face?"

Shayne nodded, taking a sip of cognac. "And about you chasing her down the back stairs and through the alley, and how she escaped from you by the skin of her teeth by hailing a cab. How'd you manage to trace her here, by the way?"

"I got the license number of the cab and found the driver and asked him. But *why* is she afraid of me, Shayne? She knows I'd never do anything to harm her." Bert Paulson looked younger than his thirty years at that moment. Young and hurt and completely bewildered.

"That's not the way she gave it to me," Shayne told him dryly. "She claims she doesn't know who you are. That she never saw you before in her life. She suspects that you murdered her brother, and—"

"Her *brother?*" Paulson's look of astonishment was ludicrous. "*I'm* her brother. Didn't she tell you that?"

Michael Shayne sat very still holding his cognac glass inches from his lips, staring into it as though he had never seen the amber stuff before and was fascinated by it.

"No," he said, slowly. "She didn't tell me that, Paulson. In fact she assured me she had seen the body of her murdered brother in room three-sixteen at the Hibiscus Hotel no less than ten minutes before you jumped at her in the corridor as she came out of the room."

Paulson's body went slack in his chair. He closed his eyes tightly and put his left hand over them as though he had to shut out the glaring overhead light. In a strangled voice, he muttered, "I guess I could use a drink after all."

Shayne poured cognac into the sherry glass on the tray. He pushed it into Paulson's hand, asking matter-of-factly, "Is it all right straight?"

Paulson sloshed a little as he got it up to his lips. He emptied the glass without taking it away, shuddered and blew out a long breath.

"I'm Nellie's brother," he told Shayne slowly. "I'm not dead, as you can well see. Now do you realize the condition she's in? Why I'm so worried? Why I have to find her and take care of her?"

Shayne said, "I can see that all right. If you *are* her brother and *are* telling the truth. But you see, I got a completely different story from her. She came here and hired me to protect her from *you*—describing you perfectly, including the scar. And she also wants me to find out who cut her brother's throat tonight and how they got rid of the body. So you can see," he ended reasonably, "it puts me in a dilemma. Until I find out which one of you is telling the truth—"

"But I can prove it," said Paulson vehemently. He reached in his hip pocket for a wallet, opened it and began pulling out cards. "I've got identification. I can prove I'm Bert Paulson. You look. I don't see too well without my glasses."

Shayne didn't glance at the cards. "And I can easily prove I'm Mike Shayne. But if I told you I had a sister named Nellie who had suddenly gone crazy and thought I was going to kill her, that wouldn't *prove* I was her brother. Pour another drink if you like, and let's hear your end of this gobbledegook."

"No, thanks. One is enough right now." Paulson put his empty glass back on the tray. "Nellie and I live in Jacksonville. That is, we did live there until I got pulled into the

Korean war. Mother died while I was overseas, and when
I came back I found Nellie living alone and apparently
liking it. She had a good job in Jax and seemed to be en-
joying being on her own."

He paused and looked down at his hands for a moment,
resuming with apparent effort. "Maybe I was wrong, but
I thought maybe it was just what she needed. Mother was
always—sort of over-possessive, I guess you'd call it. Even
with me. And Nellie never had been able to call her soul
her own. She had a nervous breakdown when she was sixteen," he went on fiercely, "and spent several months in
a sanitarium. I always felt it was entirely mother's fault.
So when I came back and thought I'd settle down in Jax
and Nellie could sort of keep house for me, I saw she re-
sented it. In fact," he went on slowly, nibbling his lower
lip in concentration, "she blew up all over the place when
I suggested it, and accused me of being as bad as mother
about wanting to hold her down.

"Well, she was twenty and earning her own living." He
spread out his hands and looked at Shayne helplessly. "I
didn't know. I loved her and wanted to protect her, but—
I just didn't know. I decided maybe it was best to let her
go it alone. So I got a job in Detroit, and from her letters I
thought everything was fine.

"That was up to two weeks ago when I got a wire saying
she was in trouble."

"What sort of trouble?"

"She didn't say. It was a funny wire. Wild and—well,
sort of incoherent. So I wired her to hold the fort and drove
down—straight through in twenty-six hours. And when I
got to Jax she'd vanished. No one knew where she had
gone. So I hired this private detective in Jacksonville, and
this afternoon he reported to me he'd located her in
Miami—at the Hibiscus Hotel. Room three-sixteen. And
I knew something was awfully funny, because always before when we came to Miami we stayed at the Tropical

Arms—where they knew us and all.

"So I jumped in my car and drove down as fast as I could."

"What time did you leave Jacksonville?" interjected Shayne.

"A little before four o'clock."

"You weren't in much of a hurry to reach her." said Shayne dryly. "Anybody can do it in four hours."

"I had an accident the other side of Fort Lauderdale. Crazy driver smashed into my rear-end when I slowed for a light."

Paulson rubbed his forehead vaguely. "Slammed me against the windshield. Broke my glasses and half knocked me out. I had to drive slow coming on in. That delayed me a couple of hours, so it was about nine-thirty when I got to the Hibiscus."

"And?" prompted Shayne when Paulson stopped again, his gaze withdrawn and inward as though the memory rankled horribly.

"Well, I went to the elevator and up to the third floor. As I walked down the corridor toward three-sixteen, I saw the door stood open and light was coming out. And when I was about eight feet away, Nellie stepped out and turned toward me. She gave one scream and started running in the other direction. I've thought and thought about it," he ended wearily, "and I admit the hall light was dim and she'd just stepped out of a brightly-lit room, so maybe she *didn't* recognize me in one glance. That might explain—"

"It wouldn't explain," said Shayne sharply, "her story about being registered at the Roney Plaza Hotel with her brother, and going to the Hibiscus at nine-thirty in response to a call from him and finding him lying on the bed in three-sixteen with his throat slit wide open."

"But there wasn't anybody in the room—dead or alive," protested Paulson. "I'm positive. I glanced in through the open door as I ran past after Nellie. The room was empty."

Shayne nodded slowly, draining his glass and setting it on the tray. "I know. That fits her story, too. About the body of her brother disappearing from the room while she was telephoning for help from another room."

"But *I'm* her brother," fumed Paulson helplessly. "Let me see her, Mr. Shayne. Let me talk to her. You can be right there and listen. Don't you see she needs help—making up a crazy story about me being murdered and then running away at the sight of me?"

"Somebody," agreed Shayne, "is sure as hell making up a crazy story." He drummed blunt fingertips on the arm of his chair indecisively. "Couple of things we can check without too much trouble."

"Then start checking them, for God's sake!" burst out Paulson. "Call yourself a detective? Get to the bottom of this. You claim Nellie is all right and you can produce her any time, but how do I know. Prove it."

Shayne said equably, "You'll have to take my word for it." He went to the telephone and called the number of the Hibiscus Hotel which he had looked up earlier. When the switchboard answered, he asked, "Do you have a Miss Paulson registered? Nellie Paulson from Jacksonville?"

"Three-sixteen," Evelyn replied at once. "But Miss Paulson isn't in just now."

"I know. Look, anything more on bodies appearing and disappearing from her room?"

There was a long pause. Then Evelyn said primly, "I'm sure I don't know what you mean, sir. Who is calling?"

Shayne said, "Never mind," and hung up. He nodded to Paulson who had risen and was looking at him eagerly. "That much checks. Miss Paulson has three-sixteen and she isn't in."

"Well—what are you waiting for?"

"One more detail." Shayne called the Roney Plaza

number from memory. He asked again, "Do you have a Miss Paulson registered? Miss Nellie Paulson from Jacksonville?"

It took quite a bit longer to get an answer this time. And it was decisively negative: "Sorry, but we have no Miss Paulson."

Shayne hung up with a shrug. He told Paulson, "I guess it's about time we tried to straighten this out." Without further explanation, he strode to the kitchen door and knocked on it. "Nellie. This is Mike Shayne. It's all right to come out now."

Bert Paulson ran toward him, his face contorted with anger. "Damn it! Do you mean to say she was in here all the time you were stalling me along? Why didn't you—?"

"Shut *up*," warned Shayne angrily. "I promised her I'd get rid of you before I called her out. If she hears you're still here—"

He turned and knocked more loudly on the door. "It's okay, Nellie. Unlock the door. I give you my word it's all right to come out."

There was still no response from the kitchen. Paulson shoved Shayne aside and rattled the knob frantically. "Nellie! Do you hear me, Nellie? It's Bert, darling. *Bert!* Don't you hear? Everything's all right. I swear it is. I've been so worried."

Shayne stood aside with a bleakly saturnine look on his face while Bert pleaded through the closed door for his sister to come out. After a few minutes attempted cajolery got them nowhere, Shayne said, "If you'd kept your damned mouth closed until she unlocked the door, everything would have been all right. As it is—the way she seems to feel about you—she's probably run out the back door and down the fire escape by this time."

"The fire escape?" Paulson whirled about, his scar standing out strongly on his cheek. "You mean there's a back way out of that room?"

Shayne said sardonically, "That's what I mean. If you'd let me handle it—"

That was as far as he got before Paulson whirled and threw his weight against the door. The hook and eye holding it on the inside gave under the impact and the door crashed open.

One glance showed them the kitchen was empty. Paulson jumped for the back door and found it unlocked, jerked it open and stepped out onto the fire escape landing to peer anxiously downward.

He reappeared with his face dark with rage. "She's gone," he panted. "God only knows where. Or what she'll do next. Damn your soul to hell, Shayne. It's *your* fault. If you'd told me at the beginning—"

Shayne caught his shoulder and whirled him about as he started to run out. "Take it easy. Maybe she had a hell of a good reason for ducking out before you broke that door down. You and I are going down to police headquarters and—"

An extraordinary change came over Bert Paulson's face. He backed away and his right hand darted inside his jacket buttoned in front and reappeared holding a Colt's .45 Army automatic aimed squarely at Shayne's belly. His lips drew away from his teeth in a wolfish grin as Shayne hesitated, trying to decide whether to jump him or not.

"Don't do it, Mister Detective. I'd just as soon kill you as any of those men I killed in Korea, and don't forget it. *You* can go down to police headquarters if you want, but you'll go alone. I've had enough talk. You don't seem to realize Nellie's out there in the night alone somewhere. With God knows what sort of hallucinations running through her head.

"I'm going out to find her, by God." He was backing away steadily toward the front door as he talked, the big gun held unwaveringly in line with Shayne's middle.

"Don't make a move forward," he warned. "Not one

step or I'll let you have it. I swear I will. She's *my* sister and I'm responsible for her."

He fumbled behind him with his left hand for the door-knob, his eyes feverishly bright on Shayne. "Don't try to follow or stop me. Somebody will sure as hell get hurt."

He opened the door and glided out, closed it behind him fast.

Shayne sighed and walked slowly to the tray and poured himself out a drink. Nellie should be perfectly safe with Lucy by this time—or at least in a cab on her way to Lucy's. And there was no possible chance for Bert to find her there. In the meantime, Shayne had a lot of questions to ask in different places.

EIGHT: *10:28 P.M.*

The girl stood inside Shayne's kitchen with her ear pressed hard against the thin wooden panel trying to hear what was going on beyond the door.

As soon as she had thrown the flimsy latch on the door behind her, she had frantically reconnoitered for a possible means of escape if it became necessary, and had unlocked and opened the back door leading out to the fire escape. With it standing invitingly open, she had returned to the other door to do her utmost to comprehend what was being said inside.

She wasn't really frightened now, she kept telling herself, trying to stop shivering as she did so. Michael Shayne's big frame and his placid way of taking things had been most reassuring. But had he believed her story? That was the crux of it. Or would he believe whatever fantastic story the man in there with him would tell to explain why he had followed her to Shayne's hotel?

She could hear only isolated words from the other room. Sometimes one or the other of them would raise his voice momentarily, and she would catch a detached phrase. But it was only gibberish that way. It didn't make sense at all.

Her mouth was dry and her heart was beating frantically and she felt faint as she clung there trying to hear.

After all, the story she had told Shayne must have sounded more like hysterical raving than the truth. Because there wasn't any way to prove a word she'd told him. Without the evidence of her brother's body to back it up—

And she had heard him call the police and the Hibiscus Hotel herself. Of course, they'd told him there was no body. She had known that already.

She stiffened as she heard one of them moving toward the kitchen door. Then there was a knock and Shayne's voice: "Nellie. This is Mike Shayne. It's all right to come out now."

And the other's voice shouting angrily as he neared the door: "Damn it! Do you mean to say she was in here all the time—?"

She waited to hear no more. She dared not hesitate longer. She whirled and slithered across the room and out the open door, drawing it silently shut behind her.

It was quite dark, but she could see the spidery iron steps leading down the single flight alongside the building to a dimly lit side street.

She went down swiftly without looking back, and at the bottom ran with all her speed toward the more brightly lighted street ahead. She had his secretary's address in her suede handbag. He had sworn she would be safe there. No matter what story he had been told, she felt she could trust him not to betray her whereabouts. He would know where she had gone as soon as he found the kitchen empty, she told herself thankfully. If she could only find a taxi now.

Reaching Southeast 2nd Avenue, she turned unhesitatingly toward the brilliantly lighted section of the city and away from the bridge across the river. She knew Flagler Street was only a block or so in this direction. There would be people and taxi stands—and safety.

She slowed to a fast walk on the avenue. There was a single loitering female figure on the sidewalk ahead of her. She had a large red handbag swinging carelessly from a strap over her shoulder and was strolling along as though she hadn't a care in the world.

And she probably hadn't, thought the distraught girl to

herself as she came up on her rapidly. Miami must be full
of people who hadn't a care in the world. Who could stroll
unconcernedly along any street in the city without fear of
pursuit. Without fear, period.

She was abreast of the other girl who turned curiously
to see who was passing in such desperate haste. She caught
only a brief glimpse of her face as she was going by without slackening her pace, and had a brief feeling of recognition.

She heard a surprised exclamation, and then the footsteps slightly behind her quickened and a moment later a
hand seized her arm firmly.

She turned to shake it off, and then she recognized the
features of the girl who had been so nice to her in the taxicab about letting the driver pick her up and take her to
Shayne's hotel.

"Goodness!" the girl exclaimed. "It is you, isn't it? I
was so utterly surprised to see you. Is everything all right?"
she went on anxiously. "Did you find your detective all
right? My, that was so exciting in the cab. Nothing ever
happens to me," she added resentfully.

Her first impulse was to rudely snatch her arm away
from the other's grasp and run on toward Flagler. But she
glanced swiftly over her shoulder at the empty street behind them, and forced herself to slow down instead. After
all, wasn't this better? Two girls walking along sedately
together. Practically running and alone as she had been,
she was much more conspicuous. And the girl *had* been
nice to her in the cab. She did owe her some explanation.
It wouldn't be very polite to brush her off now.

She caught her breath as best she could, and said, "I
never expected to see you again, either. How on earth do
you happen to be here?"

"I stopped to see a friend on Brickell the other side of
the bridge, and when I started back there weren't any
taxis. So I thought I might as well walk the few blocks."

She linked their arms together tightly as they neared the intersection, and steered the other girl across the street, saying happily, "Let's sit on a park bench for a minute and you've got to tell me all about it. You need to catch your breath anyway, and I'm just torn to pieces with curiosity. Is Michael Shayne half as attractive as they say he is—with that red hair and all?"

"Attractive?" the other asked dazedly, letting herself be led into a palm-lined path in the park, and then dropping wearily onto a bench. "Yes, I guess so. He's *nice.*"

"Why on earth were you in such a hurry to get away from him then?" purred the other.

"I—I—oh, it's all so mixed up. I don't know what to do. That man followed me there somehow, you see. And I was out in the kitchen while they talked. And I got frightened and—ran away."

"You poor thing. You mean the same man who was chasing you when you jumped in the cab with me?"

"Yes. With the scarred face. Oh, it's all so impossible I just can't make anybody understand. Even Mr. Shayne. I don't think he believed me at all."

"That's a shame. What are you going to do now?"

"He gave me an address. I've got it here in my bag. A note to his secretary where I can stay and be perfectly safe." She started up, fright seizing her anew. "I should go on. If *he* finds me here—"

The other's hand was tight on her arm, pulling her down to the bench "It's dark here. No one can see us on this bench. If he does come out looking for you, you'll be safer sitting here until he goes by than out on the street trying to find a cab. And I'm just dying to have you tell me what it's all about."

"Well, I—I guess maybe you're right." She allowed herself to be persuaded and sank back onto the bench, thinking it would be good to talk to someone else and see how her story sounded. Maybe that way it would come clearer and—

"I'm Mary Barnes," she began. "I'm staying at the Roney Plaza, and—"

It was dark on the palm-shrouded bench in the park with only a slim sliver of a moon overhead. Dark and silent except for the low murmur of the girls' voices as they sat close together.

And after a time that murmur ceased and there was complete silence for a moment, then the sound of a brief struggle and a low, gasping, "A-h-h-h."

And then more silence.

And then a single set of footsteps, coming out of the darkness and the silence to the streetlights, to wave down a cruising taxi.

And a girl getting in the rear seat and settling herself composedly in the corner and opening a black suede purse to take out a sheet of paper and read the address in Michael Shayne's handwriting aloud to the driver.

NINE: *10:34 P.M.*

The parking place in front of the Hibiscus Hotel was still empty, and Paulson parked his car there in practically the same place it had been before. He sat behind the wheel for some time before getting out, lighting a cigarette and drawing on it strongly, his features showing brooding worriment each time he sucked in.

He threw the cigarette butt away finally, and got out, indicating a certain reluctance and distaste for what he felt he must do.

He hesitated beside the car for a moment, reaching inside his coat to settle the Army automatic snugly and inconspicuously against his left groin and checking to see that his coat was buttoned over it. Then he squared his shoulders and went toward the lighted entrance to the hotel.

The clerk was behind the desk, leaning on his elbows with his sharp chin cupped in his hands. Beyond him, Paulson saw Evelyn's profile in front of her switchboard, a discontented frown on her rather pretty face as she contemplated the sickening waste of these two hours during which she might just as well have been with Roger.

At the elevator beyond the desk, the operator lounged outside the open door of his car in conversation with the only bellboy in sight.

It all looked completely dull and normal, not at all as though there had been any murders or alarms of murder recently, and Paulson was encouraged to cross to the desk casually and lean one elbow on it in a negligent sort of way when Dick snapped to attention behind it.

"Do you have a Miss Paulson registered here?" Paulson forestalled Dick's automatic motion of reaching for the registry pad and a pen.

Dick said, "Yes, sir, we do," looking at the tall man and his scarred face with intense interest.

"Is she in now?"

"No, sir. I'm afraid she isn't."

"Any reason why you should be so sure without trying her room?"

Dick permitted himself a faint smile. There were several very good reasons why he was certain that the occupant of 316 was not in her room, but he had no intention of revealing them to this stranger. With a trace of hauteur, he said. "I'm quite sure she's out. However, there's a house phone if you wish to call her room."

Paulson shook his head. "Any idea when she'll be in?"

"None."

Paulson ostentatiously grimaced at this. "I'm her brother," he explained carefully. "Just drove in from Jacksonville to see Nellie on a rather important matter. She had promised to be here when I arrived."

"I see. I'm very sorry, but—" Dick smiled thinly. Her brother? He wondered.

Paulson shrugged. "Doubtless she'll be in soon. I'm tired after a long drive. I suppose it'll be all right if I go up to her room to wait for her?"

Dick hesitated. Normally, he would not have refused such a request—whether the man in question pretended to be her brother or not. After all, the Hibiscus was no different from any other respectable, middle-class hotel. They didn't attempt to ride herd on the morals of their guests. Nellie Paulson had had other men visitors in her room during her two-week stay.

But the situation tonight was not quite normal. There was that unexplained telephone call at nine-thirty which either had or hadn't stated there was a murdered man in

Miss Paulson's room—depending on whether Evelyn had misunderstood 316 for 360 or not. And there was the more recent call from outside (promptly reported by Evelyn) inquiring about bodies disappearing from 316.

He said, "I'm afraid that would be quite against our rules, sir. We'll be very glad to have you make yourself comfortable here in the lobby while you wait."

Paulson smiled and said quietly, "I wouldn't blame you for taking that attitude if I weren't her brother. But I am, and I can prove it." He got out his wallet and withdrew an insurance identification card which he laid on the desk.

Dick glanced at it and nodded slowly. It looked all right. He said, "It wasn't that I doubted your word, sir. It's just that we do have these rules." He hesitated a moment. With everything that had happened, he decided Ollie had better take the responsibility of this. He handed the card back and said briskly, "Perhaps you'd like to speak to our Mr. Patton. I really don't have the authority—" He turned his head to Evelyn, "Ask Mr. Patton to step out here a moment, please."

Evelyn's eyes were rounded on Paulson's scarred face as she obeyed. What was this all about? She hadn't been able to overhear the conversation at the desk, but anything that needed Ollie's attention might prove very interesting. What with dead bodies that weren't there and all, maybe she wasn't going to mind missing her date with Roger so much after all.

Paulson nodded pleasantly at Dick's suggestion, negligently lit a cigarette and waited. When Patton came around the corner from his office, Dick introduced Paulson and explained the situation briefly.

The sleepiness went away from Patton's eyes as he listened. He studied Paulson carefully and nodded, took him by the arm to turn him toward his office and said, "If you'll just step this way, Mr. Paulson, there's a couple of questions I'd like to ask you."

Paulson went with him willingly, though he protested, "This is the damndest hocus-pocus I ever ran into about waiting for my sister in her room. I showed the clerk my identification."

"Sure, sure," said Patton soothingly, holding the door of his office open for Paulson to precede him inside. "No one doubts you're her brother. Just sit down there and tell me something about your sister, Mr. Paulson."

"What sort of things?" demanded Paulson tensely. "Has anything happened to Nellie?"

"Not that we know of. It's just that something real funny happened tonight that maybe has some connection with her. U-m-m, would you say she's much of a practical joker?"

"Nellie? Not to my knowledge. No more than anyone. She's got a good sense of humor, but— What the devil are you getting at?"

"Does she ever—uh—well, have hallucinations, sort of?" Patton probed delicately. "Maybe take a drink too many sometimes and see things when they ain't there?" He laughed lightly to take any possible sting away from the question, but Paulson's face clouded with anger.

"I don't like these insinuations about my sister. Tell me straight out what you're talking about."

Oliver Patton sighed. There wasn't very much to tell, actually. They had no proof whatsoever that it had been Nellie Paulson who made the phone call from 360. Indeed, there was evidence that she could not have made it, for Dick thought he recalled seeing her go out some time previous to the call, and she hadn't shown up in the hotel since it happened.

So he said placatingly, "The way it looks then is that someone else was trying to play a joke on her. Calling downstairs to say there was a dead man in her room."

Paulson's face expressed complete surprise. "A dead man in Nellie's room?" he gasped as though this were the first he'd heard of such a thing. "When? Who was he?"

Patton waved a fat hand. "There wasn't anybody as a matter of fact. I checked right away, of course, and that's why I say it must have been a joke of some sort. But we got to check every angle of a thing like that. That's why I asked what sort of girl your sister is. Whether she's the type to pull a practical joke."

Paulson shook his head decidedly. "She isn't." He paused, looking away from Patton and seeming to nerve himself to speak further. "On the other hand, I—now that you've brought it up, maybe you'll tell *me* something. I don't suppose it has anything to do with what happened here tonight," he went on hastily, "but I'm afraid she has been running sort of wild and getting mixed up with some-queer characters recently. At home, that is. In Jacksonville. So maybe you could tell me something about how she's been conducting herself here. Whether she's—uh—been running around much. With men, you know? Any special man particularly."

Patton hesitated, rubbing the third fold of fat beneath his chin and studying Paulson speculatively. "It isn't the sort of information we're supposed to hand out about our guests. This ain't the F.B.I., you know. We don't keep any dossier on our guests."

"I know that," said Paulson impatiently. "but I also know something about the way hotels are run. The bell-boys and the maids and the clerk. They always know pretty well what's going on. Whether there're late parties and how many drinks they take up, and who has visitors and how long they stay. That sort of stuff." He smiled winningly at Patton. "You're the house detective, aren't you? Don't tell me you didn't ask around and check up on my sister's conduct during the past two weeks when this thing happened tonight."

Patton clasped his hands together in front of his paunch and looked down at them studiously. "I wouldn't say I didn't. But it still isn't the kind of information we give out."

Paulson grimaced and got out his wallet. He half withdrew a ten and glanced covertly at Patton, then sighed and made it a twenty instead. He folded the bill lengthwise four times and said, "I wouldn't expect you to give it out to anyone except her brother. But I certainly have a perfect right to know. I tell you I've been worried about the way she's been acting—and now with this thing tonight—and her not being here to meet me as she promised—"

Patton unclasped his hands from in front of his paunch, and the bill was whisked out of sight. He said, "Sure. Being her brother and all, I guess it wouldn't be right not to tell you.

"Well, your sister has been mighty pleasant and quiet in the hotel, and minds her own business. I did go over the room service charges on her bill tonight, and most nights she's had ice and sometimes soda up. A bottle of whisky twice in two weeks." He spread out his hand. "No, I'm not denying the bellboys and maids, like you say, notice things that go on. They can't help it, having eyes and being human. But the way I get it, your sister has entertained men frequently, but never too late. And never no commotion or trouble at all. Just the sort of thing any nice, attractive girl in a hotel in Miami on her own might be expected to do."

He nodded benignly at Paulson. "Mostly one particular fellow, the way I get it. With maybe a couple others off and on. But she minds her own business, and so do they. She paid up her first week's bill promptly and we haven't any complaints at all. That the sort of stuff you wanted to know?"

Paulson wet his lips and nodded. "Exactly. Thanks, Mr. Patton." He arose. "And now is it all right for me to go up to her room to wait?"

Patton arose with him. "Sure. I'll go up and let you in myself. Give me a chance to check around a little more to be plumb certain she hasn't got any bodies concealed. That's strictly against the rules, you know." He winked jovially at his own joke. "And then I reckon I might just as well wait there with you until she does come in. Ask her a couple of questions there in private, just to get everything real clear."

Paulson said, "That'll be fine. Glad to have company while I wait for Nellie."

They went out and strolled toward the elevator together, and Paulson stopped abruptly in mid-stride. "It's getting so late maybe I'd better get my baggage and check into a room of my own. Take me half an hour perhaps. I had a little accident outside of town and had to leave my car at a garage. If Nellie comes in before I get back, tell her to stay put, will you?"

"Sure."

Oliver Patton fidgeted painfully on his bunion-infested feet and watched Paulson's tall figure striding across the lobby with a speculative frown. Maybe it wasn't anything, but the young fellow had appeared to lose interest abruptly in waiting in his sister's room when Patton suggested that he would go up and wait with him. And it was funny the way he suddenly remembered that he hadn't got his baggage with him and decided to go fetch it. Why hadn't he thought about that when he left his car? He must have known he'd be spending the night at some hotel in town and would be needing it.

Starting to turn back to his office, Patton saw Bill signal to him from where he stood beside the open elevator. He plodded across to him and Bill said eagerly:

"Joe, here, swears he's seen that guy in here before. Some time this evening, he thinks, but he's not sure."

"That's right, Chief." Joe scratched his head dubiously. "I know I've seen him. In the elevator, I reckon. Seems

like I noticed him special because I thought he was trying
to hold the scarred side of his face away from me. Like
maybe he didn't want to be recognized."

"This evening?" demanded Patton tautly.

"I just don't disremember for sure," groaned Joe. "You
know how it is, Mr. Oliver. Up and down. Down and up.
You don't really notice. But that man with the scar on his
face—he's been in this here elevator last day or so, and
that's a fact."

Patton said, "Let me know if he shows up again." He
went to the desk and gave the same instructions to Dick.
"And have Evvie give me an open wire if he calls, or if
anybody calls for Miss Paulson."

Then, remindful of Mike Shayne's previous interest in
the girl, he lumbered back to his office to telephone .the
red-headed detective. Unfortunately, Shayne's telephone
was not answered.

TEN: *10:34 P.M.*

Before starting out to look for answers, Michael Shayne telephoned Lucy.

Her voice was acidly sweet as she replied in mock surprise, "Not finished with the blonde so *soon,* Michael?"

"All finished," he told her cheerfully, "so I decided to sick her onto you. She's not there yet?"

There was a tiny pause, during which he knew Lucy was trying to decide whether he was kidding or serious. Then she said, "Not yet."

"She should be showing shortly. Be nice to her, angel. She's really in a state."

"Because you got rid of her so fast?"

Shayne growled, "This is serious, Lucy. Her name is Nellie Paulson—at least, I guess maybe it is. I don't know whether she's actually nuts or not, but she's on the fringe. Scared out of her wits. There's a guy out on the town hunting her with a gun who claims he's her brother and wants to take care of her. But *she* claims this guy murdered her brother and is after her now."

Lucy said pleasantly, "What interesting people you do meet, Mr. Shayne. Just what am I supposed to do with this damsel who doesn't know whether her brother is a murderer or murderee?"

"Just keep her quiet there and take care of her," growled Shayne. "Put her to bed if you can. And don't let anyone get to her. Call me as soon as she gets there," he added hastily. "I'll be at police headquarters. In Gentry's office, if he's still there; if not, check with Sergeant Jenkins."

Lucy said, "Yes, Michael," in a subdued tone. Then, "And—Michael?"

"Yes?"

"Your glass of brandy is still sitting here and it's—still an hour and twenty-five minutes until midnight."

"Save it," he said blithely. "Our date is still on."

He hung up and got his hat, went down to drive directly to Miami police headquarters.

Will Gentry was still in his private office. He was closeted there with Timothy Rourke, reporter on the *News* and one of Shayne's oldest friends in the city.

Will Gentry was a big, square man, with a florid, open countenance. He sat behind a wide, bare desk, chewing vigorously on the short butt of a black cigar; while Rourke was tilted back in a straight chair against the wall, just finishing what he considered an extremely funny story, as Shayne walked in.

"—And so the gink said, 'What cow are you talking about?' " concluded Rourke, and began laughing uproariously.

Chief Gentry said, "Ha-ha," while looking at Shayne. "Anything up, Mike?"

"He is, damn it," said Rourke. "Just in time to spoil the point of my story. Thought you had a date with Lucy tonight?"

"I did. A blonde came between us." Shayne grinned at him and pulled a chair close to Gentry's desk. "Had any unexplained corpses tonight, Will?"

"No corpses of any sort. You?"

"I'll be damned if I know," said Shayne, feelingly. "Had any sort of report of trouble at the Hibiscus Hotel?"

"I don't think so." Gentry looked at the reporter. "You had anything, Tim?"

"Not a thing all evening to make the Night Edition." Rourke tilted his chair forward so all four legs were on the floor, leaned his cadaverous body forward eagerly.

"Got something, Mike?"

"I'll still be damned if I know. Let's see what you two master-minds make out of this. Lucy and I had just settled down at her place for a night-cap when the clerk at my hotel phoned me—"

Shayne went on to tell about his return to the hotel, his first brief encounter with the young woman in the lobby who was so eager for him to take on an immediate tailing job, and his interview with the other girl upstairs. He omitted only the fact that he had given the girl a note to Lucy and told her to go there, ending the first part of his story with her locking herself in the kitchen while he admitted the man with the scar on his face.

"So, what do you make of it thus far?" he demanded.

Chief Gentry took the soggy cigar butt from his mouth and regarded it with intense distaste. With the easy and unthinking accuracy of a major-league shortstop throwing to first, he tossed it aside into a brass spittoon in one corner. "The Hibiscus should have notified us," he growled, reaching for a button on his desk. "I'll get Patton in and—"

"Wait a minute, Will. You know Ollie. He's okay. But he's got a job. If your damned pensions were big enough to support a man, he wouldn't have, but they aren't and so he gets paid a salary to keep things as quiet as he can for the hotel. You know that," remonstrated Shayne. "What was there for him to report? He found no evidence of murder."

"All right," said Gentry. "Sure, Ollie's okay, but these hotel dicks are always covering up. Was the girl drunk or nuts?"

"Not drunk," said Shayne. "Nuts, maybe. How do you tell? Her story sounded straight enough when she was telling it."

"Yeh? Then how did her scarred face friend follow her to your place? According to her, she left him standing in the street while she went off in a taxi without knowing where she was headed."

"He explained to me that he caught the number of her taxi, went to the company's office and got her destination from the driver over their radio system."

"Could be," said Gentry shortly. "What sort of story did *he* tell? Cut out this continued-in-our-next stuff."

Shayne grinned cheerily and said, "That's what you call a cliff-hanger. All right. *He* claims *he's* her brother. And that she's half nuts and screamed and ran away from him the moment she saw him in the hotel corridor."

"Was this scar a fresh one, by any chance?" asked Tim Rourke with interest. "One that just healed up this evening?"

"It looks more like one from Korea," Shayne said briefly. He went on to relate everything Bert Paulson had told him about the inexplicable affair, ending at the point where he had pulled an ex-Army gun on Shayne and gone storming out into the Miami night to search for his sister.

"And you let him walk out just like that?" demanded Rourke incredulously. "Knowing how terrified she was of him?"

Without revealing that he felt she would be perfectly safe with Lucy Hamilton, Shayne scowled at the reporter and asked, "How many slap-happy ex-G.I.'s have you gone up against while they had forty-fives in their fists?"

Rourke shrugged his thin shoulders. "That's why I'm a reporter instead of pretending to be a detective. Look, Mike." His voice became reflective. "Did you say Paulson? Bert Paulson? From Jacksonville, huh?"

"That's what he said. Offered identification cards to prove it."

Both Shayne and Gentry remained silent while Tim Rourke rocked back in his chair again, carefully placed the tips of ten fingers against each other in front of his nose and studied them with a frown. They both respected his encyclopedic knowledge of current affairs as reported in the newspapers and his prodigious memory, and they waited to see if he could dredge anything up for them.

"Paulson? Yeh. Hell, it's been quite recent. Last two or three weeks. Jacksonville?" He closed his eyes a moment in fierce concentration, then snapped his fingers excitedly.

"Got it! Badger game. Girl named Nellie Paulson and her brother. Only they tried it on the wrong sucker two weeks ago and he called cops. It wasn't much of a splash. Just a couple of lines in the *News* here, but there was a description of both of them. They both got clean away," he went on. "Beat it fast when the guy refused to pay off. Jax should have a pick-up out on them," he added to Gentry.

"Doubt if they'd bother," he grunted, leaning forward to open the inter-com on his desk and speak into it. "Those badger games are hard to pin down. Ninety-nine times out of a hundred the sucker refuses to prefer charges."

"I don't believe it," Shayne told Rourke flatly.

He shrugged thin shoulders. "Come up to the morgue with me and I'll find the paper. Why do you doubt me?"

"The girl mostly. She may be nuts, but I'll be damned if I can see her playing the badger game. And her brother! Damn it, have you forgotten he says he was in Detroit until two weeks ago?"

"Maybe he made a special trip back to shake down a sucker she had lined up."

Shayne said, "Maybe. But that sure as hell wasn't the way he told it to me."

"Would you expect a guy to tell you about a badger game he'd been pulling with his sister as decoy?" Rourke demanded acidly.

A voice came over the inter-com and they all listened intently to a report from the records room that no Paulson was currently listed as wanted.

"There you are," said Shayne. "For once, Tim, your vaunted memory—"

"My vaunted memory is exactly what it's vaunted to be," snapped Rourke. "Will is right. The Jax police probably didn't bother to put out a pick-up, knowing there wouldn't be a conviction. But you call them, Chief, if you want to verify it."

Gentry looked inquiringly at Shayne.

He nodded angrily. "Check on it, for God's sake! This thing has got me going around in circles. If the girl and her brother are mixed up in something like that it changes everything."

Chief Gentry spoke into the inter-com again. Then he leaned back in his swivel chair and took another thick, black cigar from his breast pocket, sniffed it hopefully and bit off the end.

"How does it change everything, Mike?" he asked absently. "You've still got the two of them telling diametrically opposed stories. You've still got a corpse that isn't there—a hysterical girl who doesn't recognize her own brother—"

He struck a match and put flame to the end of his cigar, contentedly puffed out a billow of black smoke.

"If they're mixed up in something like that," said Shayne. "I'd say she might have recognized him in the corridor and that's why she ran. Maybe they had a fight in Jax and he's out to get her. All that other stuff she told me—maybe that was just window-dressing—just to befog the issue because she didn't want to admit it was her own brother whom she was deathly afraid of."

"But you said," Rourke reminded him maliciously, "that she saw her brother's body and reported it over another phone *before* her brother jumped her. And Patton verified that when you called him."

"Yeh," Shayne agreed sourly. He angrily ran knobby fingers through his coarse hair and demanded, "Why do these screwy things have to happen to me? Why in the goddam hell can't I for just once in my life get a nice, high-priced, clean-cut sort of case like I used to handle back in World-Wide?"

"Because," Rourke told him cheerily, "you've got all the taxi drivers in town capping for you and steering clients your way. And you'd turn it down cold if you did get one," he continued happily. "Look at tonight for instance. You have this well-stacked babe proposition you on a nice, high-priced, clean-cut sort of tailing case, and what do you do? Turn her down cold, of course. Why? Because you've got a great big black Irish hunch that something more interesting is waiting for you upstairs. So-o-o. Now you're in the middle of it, and here you are complaining."

There was a knock on the door and a uniformed man entered with a sheet of paper. He laid it on the desk in front of Gentry, saying, "The information you wanted from Jacksonville, sir."

Gentry laid his cigar aside and picked it up. He glanced through it and told Shayne placidly, "Tim was correct as usual. Bert and Nellie Paulson. Thirty-one and twenty-two respectively." He glanced on across the typed lines, muttering, "Blonde. Five-feet-four. Hundred eighteen. Brown hair. Five-ten. Hundred-fifty."

He paused a moment, frowned, and then put the sheet down. "Nothing here about a scar on his face, Mike. It's a pretty complete description otherwise."

Shayne's jaw was set and the trenches showed deeply in his cheeks. "Did I hear you read that right? Height five-ten and weight a hundred-fifty?"

Gentry referred to the sheet again. He nodded. "That's right. And no scar."

"So he was lying," Shayne said thickly. "He's not Bert Paulson at all."

"Guess not," said Gentry cheerfully. "Here's something else. It says they have evidence this isn't the first of these stunts the Paulson brother-and-sister team have pulled. Two others in the past three months that didn't get re-

ported until this was in the papers. Didn't your Bert
Paulson tell you he'd been living in Detroit and just came
down in answer to a wire from his sister?"

Shayne nodded grimly. "That's what he told me."

"And now he's gone out with a gun looking for her,"
said Gentry sharply. "Could be he's one of her victims that
finally decided to get sore."

The telephone on Chief Gentry's desk rang just then.
He answered it, said, "Hi, honey," after a moment, and
extended it to Shayne. "Your ever-loving and long-suffer-
ing secretary on the wire, Mr. Shayne."

He took it and Lucy said, "She's here, Mike. You told
me to call you."

"Swell." He made his voice light and bantering. "You
just keep it right there until I get around. Before midnight as I promised."

He hung up and grinned. "Just reminding me she's
still got that drink of cognac poured out and waiting for
me."

ELEVEN: *10:46 P.M.*

Lucy Hamilton sat stiffly erect in a straight chair near the telephone in her living room, smoking a cigarette and frowning a little, half-closing her eyes against the blue smoke that curled lazily up from the tip of the white cylinder in her left hand.

Each time she opened her eyes, her gaze went across the room to the big chair beside the sofa and the low table beside it with the glasses and cognac bottle she had set out for her red-headed employer more than an hour previously.

The untouched glasses mocked at her. Her brown eyes smarted each time she looked at them, and she blinked them shut to keep back the tears.

It was silly of her to feel this way, of course. This was no different from many other times. Tonight was just an integral part of the pattern she had cut out for her future when she went to work as Michael Shayne's secretary. For years, she had accepted the pattern. She accepted it now. But, damn it! Tonight—

The fingertips of her right hand drummed restlessly on the telephone stand beside her. Until his telephone call a few minutes ago she had been not too unhappily quiescent, waiting for him to return so they could have a drink together.

Tonight? Somehow, tonight had been different. Michael had seemed subtly different as they drove home together after a perfect shore dinner. With her face pressed against his shoulder in the car she had allowed herself to drift away once again on the wings of a recurring dream. It wasn't often she allowed herself to do that. Not these days. Not after these years of being with Michael. Of working so closely with him.

Always, there would be a telephone to take him from her side. Her right hand clenched into a tight fist. That was the pattern. His work came first. Any blonde floozy who had got herself in trouble and wanted him to get her out of it would always come first with Michael. Damn her anyway!

And now he was pulling Lucy into it with him. She had been sitting beside the telephone like this ever since Shayne had phoned to say he was sending his latest blonde over to her place for her to hold the girl's hand.

So, he didn't know whether she was "actually nuts" or not? And Lucy was supposed to bed down this blonde half-wit and keep her quiet and entertained while Shayne went off on a tangent hunting a brother who might not be a brother after all because *she* said her brother had been murdered—

God!

Her buzzer sounded from the push-button in the foyer downstairs. Lucy got up and went to the door and unhooked the receiver and spoke into the mouthpiece: "Yes? Who is it?"

"Miss Hamilton?" The voice was flat and metallic in her ear.

"Yes."

"This is— I've a note for you from Mr. Shayne."

Lucy said coldly, "I know. He telephoned for me to expect you. I'm on the first floor." She pressed the button that released the catch on the inside door below. She held it a long moment, then released it and opened her door, stepped out on the landing and listened to the clack of high heels ascending the stairs.

She stood there and watched, saw the top of a blonde head of hair appear over the railing, then a pretty young face that was tilted upward anxiously. A timid smile fluttered on red lips when the girl saw her waiting on the landing. She came on up, clutching a black suede handbag nervously and said, "Miss Hamilton? I—I know this is an awful intrusion at this time of night, but Mr. Shayne said—"

"I know just about what Mr. Shayne said," Lucy assured her dryly. "It's all part of my job—giving succor to his frightened female clients. Go on in."

She stood back composedly and let the girl precede her into the lighted room, closed the door firmly and made sure it was double-locked, then turned slowly to look at her visitor.

She had stopped in the center of the long room and stood there with her back to Lucy. For a moment, her young shoulders slumped forlornly, and Lucy had to fight back a sudden up-welling of sympathy. She didn't want to feel sympathetic, damn it! She wanted to hate the girl who had taken Michael away from her on this particular night.

When the girl just kept on standing there with her back turned, Lucy moved toward her, saying calmly, "So, you're Miss Paulson? May I call you Nellie?"

The girl whirled about at the words, her features twisting strangely, her eyes wild, and Shayne's warning came sharply to Lucy: *I don't know whether she's actually nuts or not, but she's on the fringe.*

"On the fringe" was putting it mildly, Lucy thought to herself as the girl demanded, "How did you know—who told you my name was Nellie Paulson?"

"Mr. Shayne. When he telephoned me."

"Oh—I see." The distorted features smoothed out slowly. She even managed a smile as she fumbled with the catch of her black bag and got it open, extracted a sheet of paper and held it out to Lucy. "Here's the note he wrote for you. Just so you'll know."

Lucy glanced at the note and found it was about what

she had expected. In the meantime, the girl turned away
from her to the sofa, removing her jacket as she did so.
"You've got a drink all poured out for me," she breathed
happily, reaching for the cognac glass waiting for
Shayne's return. "I can use one right now—believe me.
After all I've been through."

"Not that one!" said Lucy sharply.

She drew her hand back from the wine-glass as though
it had burned her, and looked up in perplexity. "Sorry. I
thought you'd fixed it for me."

Now her lips were pouting and she looked like a little
girl about to cry after her favorite doll had been snatched
away from her, Lucy thought despondently. "Dear God.
What has Michael let me in for this time?"

Aloud, she said hurriedly, "You're welcome to a drink,
of course. It's just that— I'll get you another glass." She
went swiftly into the kitchen and returned with a clean
glass, and her cheeks were rosy as she confessed, "I'm just
sort of superstitious, I guess. I'd poured that for Mr. Shayne
when he was called out to see you, and he promised to be
back to drink it with me before midnight."

"Before midnight?" her visitor echoed speculatively,
watching avidly as Lucy poured out another drink, and
glancing down at her wristwatch.

"Not that I believe for a moment he'll make it." Lucy
shrugged and reached for her tumbler where she had
poured an inch of cognac more than an hour before. The
ice cubes were more than half-melted now, and the diluted
liquor in the glass was a pale amber. She moved to the
other end of the sofa with it, and the girl took a tentative
sip of her drink and sputtered doubtfully, "It's awfully
strong, isn't it?"

"I don't like it straight," Lucy confessed. "I'll get you
some water or soda if you like."

"That's okay, I guess. I'll just sip it slowly. How much
—did Mr. Shayne tell you about me over the phone?"

"Not very much. Just that some awful man is chasing you with a gun, and you're frightened and I'm not to let anyone in. So you needn't be worried any more," Lucy went on practically. "I'm quite sure Michael will take care of everything."

"Oh, I'm sure he will, too," the girl agreed fervently. "He's really wonderful, isn't he? Mr. Shayne? It must be marvelous to work for him. So exciting and interesting."

"It's very seldom dull," Lucy conceded dryly. "Now look. I don't want to pry, and I know you're all upset and must be terribly worried about your brother."

She had managed that very well, Lucy thought complacently. Whether the brother had been murdered as Shayne said the girl believed, or whether it was her brother who was chasing her—Lucy felt she had made the statement sufficiently ambiguous to cover either contingency.

"So if you just want to sit here quietly and not talk about it at all, it's perfectly all right with me," Lucy went on evenly. "And if you want to lie down after you've finished your drink, there's an extra bed all made up. The most important thing is to relax and try to forget all about it. We can just pretend we're old friends and you've dropped in for a chat, and talk about—well, ships and shoes and sealing wax and such."

She received a humbly grateful look in return. "And cabbages and kings, maybe? But—didn't he tell you anything about what happened at the Hibiscus Hotel tonight?"

"Not a single thing. You can, if you wish, but don't feel you have to. *I'm* not a detective and not a bit of good in the world at deductions."

"I guess you're right. I guess I should just try to put it all out of my mind. Do you think Mr. Shayne *will* be back for his drink before midnight?"

"Not unless he finishes up whatever he's doing first. You know better than I what that is."

Lucy sat erect suddenly as she finished speaking, and leaned forward to put her glass down. "I forgot. I promised to call him as soon as you got here."

She went to the telephone and dialed a number, and when a male voice replied, she said:

"I'd like Chief Gentry's office, please. If he's still at headquarters."

TWELVE: *10:52 P.M.*

From the yacht basin in Biscayne Bay, Miami's sky-line at night is brilliantly lighted and imposing. Water-front hotels rise sheerly and almost solidly from the western shore of the bay, their windows glittering with thousands of lights that are reflected from the placid surface of the water.

During the Season, the basin is crowded with hundreds of varied hulls anchored close together in serried ranks: from the huge luxury yachts of millionaires to sleek, twenty-foot launches sleeping two in cramped quarters.

At this period in early autumn, only a dozen or so craft were anchored in the basin. One of them was a slim forty-foot sailing vessel named the *Marjie J.* She rode silently at anchor with riding lights fore and aft, and in her bow there were also the companionable lights of two cigarettes gleaming on and off quite close together.

One of the cigarettes shone long and brightly and then described an arc over the side and died with a hiss in the water. Muriel stretched indolently in her deck chair, and her left hand gripped her companion's trailing fingers tightly.

"Darling," she sighed, "I must go back."

"It's still early," he protested, just as indolently. He held up a bare muscular forearm to study the radium dial of his watch. "Not even eleven." His hand tightened on hers between the two deck chairs. "I thought we'd go down to the cabin again—before you took off."

"Please, Norman." She drew her hand from his and sat

up, looking toward the magnificent sky-line of the Magic City, with furrowed forehead. "You know John comes home early sometimes. I must get back."

Norman said, "Oh, damn John. Suppose he does come home and find you out? He won't know where you've been."

"He'd have his suspicions." She kept her voice light, but there was an underlying note of gravity. "We shouldn't do this, Norman. It isn't right."

"But it's nice." He sat up suddenly and showed white teeth in the faint moonlight. "You won't deny that."

"While it's happening," she said flatly. She got to her feet, a tall, well-boned woman of thirty-five, wearing a thin skirt that whipped about her thighs in the light in-shore breeze. "Afterward, you don't have to lie in bed beside John and think how it would be if he ever found out."

"No," he agreed amiably. "I'm spared that." He swung to his feet beside her, bronzed body wearing only skin-tight bathing trunks. He put one arm about her tightly and nuzzled his lips in her hair, turning her slowly and tipping up her face for a long kiss.

Her arms went about him passionately, and sharp finger-nails clawed at the flesh of his bare back, not hard enough to draw blood but leaving streaks of whiteness behind them when they fell away limply.

He lifted his head and smiled down at her upturned face and whispered huskily, "Still want to go back?"

"No." Her voice was as husky as his. "But we must." She turned away with determination and made her way back to the stern where a skiff's painter was looped about a cleat, and Norman followed her reluctantly.

"If we must, we must," he said with as much cheeriness as he could muster, loosening the line and drawing the skiff close beneath the graceful, over-hung hull and help-ing her down into it.

She seated herself in the stern, and he leaped down lightly, settled oars in the locks and rowed toward the shore lights.

There was a faint phosphorescent gleam on the placid surface of the bay, and the only sound was a little sluffing of water against the bow, the occasional splash of an oar as he sent the boat skimming over the surface with powerful strokes.

Neither of them spoke until half the distance was covered. She was thinking of her husband and of their lost love with a sad sort of nostalgia, and he was thinking about the solid night's sleep he was going to enjoy alone aboard the *Marjie J.* after he dropped her at the dock and returned.

"Norman! Be careful." Her voice was a sudden gasp and she half rose, pointing over his shoulder with a trembling forefinger.

He twisted his head to look just as the bow struck solidly against a floating object.

There was a dull, curiously sodden thud. The skiff lost way and floated aimlessly as they both stared in frightened fascination at the floating body of a dead man.

"My God," said Norman, shipping an oar hastily to revolve the stern. "It's a corpse, Muriel. A man. Here, take this other oar and bring me back close. I'll get in the bow and try to drag him in."

"Do you have to, Norman?" Her voice was thin with terror. "Can't we just—leave him? Someone else will find him. Why us? You'll have to report to the police. They'll take our names. No, Norman! We mustn't."

"Cut it out, Muriel." His voice was crisp with annoyance. "Get that oar in the water. We're drifting away. Of course, we have to. But don't worry. You can get in your car and drive away before I report it. No one will know I wasn't taking a midnight row alone."

He knelt in the bow and directed her efforts with the

oar. "A little more to my left—now forward. Hold it." He leaned far over and got a grip of water-soaked coat, tugged and lifted and grunted, and gradually drew the dead weight upward and over the edge where it plopped to the bottom of the boat in a crumpled heap bearing little semblance to a human body.

"That does it." Norman sank back on his knees, breathing hard. He leaned over the heap of water-logged flesh and muttered, "Poor devil's throat is slashed wide open."

He turned about to resume his rowing seat and take up the oars, looking on in silent commiseration while Muriel leaned over and retched agonizingly.

"Just don't think about it," he counseled. "It's nothing to do with us. We'll be at the pier in a jiffy, and you get in your car and drive straight home and forget this happened. I'll have to find some joint that's open where I can telephone from, and you'll be absolutely in the clear."

She sat with bowed head, trembling a little, and did not answer him. She couldn't explain to him that it had come to her suddenly that the man in the water might have been some woman's husband—some woman who perhaps had found illicit love more exciting and more zestful than the tamer caresses he could offer her—a man whose name might be John.

It was a bizarre and inexplicable thought, and it made her weep silently as she sat in the boat with bowed head until it came up to the end of a deserted fishing pier.

And Norman saw the tears on her cheeks as he tied up the boat and awkwardly helped her out; and wondered what the hell had got into her, when she broke away from him with a little cry as he tried to comfort her.

He stood and watched her run down the pier to the place where she'd left her car parked when he met her earlier, and then he followed more slowly, giving her plenty of time to drive away from the spot before he reported his discovery to the police. And he had no way in the world of knowing that his affair with Muriel was already ended, and he never did understand why it was that she resolutely refused to speak to him every time he tried to telephone her in the following days.

THIRTEEN: *11:00 P.M.*

When Shayne put the telephone down after Lucy's call, he strode back and forth across the office rumpling his hair angrily. "Let's try to make a little sense out of all this. Let's see what we *know* at the moment."

He stopped and held up one finger for each item as he said it aloud:

"First. The man who told me he was Bert Paulson—who had a wallet with Paulson's identification—isn't Paulson. He doesn't answer the description from Jax, and though he's trying to pose as Paulson, he evidently doesn't know that Nellie's brother has been living with her in Jacksonville all along. Else why would he have bothered with a story about working in Detroit and just coming down two weeks ago in answer to a wire from her?"

He glared at Gentry and Rourke as he frowned at his own question. "Well, why did he tell me that? Damn it, if he does know about Nellie's trouble in Jax—and he must because he said he hired a private detective to locate her—then he must know she pulled the badger game there with her brother, and it ruins his chance of getting by with impersonating Paulson by adding the Detroit touch. So why do it?"

"You tell us, Mike," Will Gentry said cheerfully. "Right now this is your baby from the word go."

Shayne said, "All right. That's one thing we know for certain. That he isn't Paulson. Now, let's see what we actually know about Nellie.

"Fact number two. She evidently *didn't* lie about being

frightened in the Hibiscus by some man *not* her brother.
Their two stories agree on that one point—other than the
mix-up in relationship. But what about the dead body she
claims she saw? Her brother with his throat cut?"

"The body that isn't there any more?" Tim Rourke put
in.

"Yeh. But we have proof that she did call down to report
a body. At least, someone called down from three-sixty.
Oliver Patton backs up that much of her story. Why would
anybody do a crazy thing like that if there wasn't a body?"

"I think the crux of the whole matter lies in one word
you just used," said Gentry placidly. "Crazy. If the girl's
off her rocker, there's no use trying to find a reasonable
motivation for anything she says or does."

"But damn it, Will. I don't believe that girl's crazy.
Scared and hysterical—sure. But I talked with her for ten
minutes. She acted exactly as I'd expect a girl to act who'd
been through exactly the harrowing experience she described."

"You're not a doctor," said Gentry impatiently. "I think
we better put out a pick-up on both of them, Mike. Sit
down and write out the best description you can of both
of them. I'll put it on the radio to all cars."

Shayne shrugged and sat down and drew a sheet of paper
toward him. He scribbled swiftly on it for several minutes,
then shoved it toward Gentry. Knowing the girl was safely
parked in Lucy's apartment was his ace-in-the-hole now.
He didn't want her picked up for questioning yet, but he
didn't mind her description going out on an All Cars because he knew they'd never find her. And he did want the
scarred-face man picked up.

Will Gentry read the two descriptions over the inter-
com, and was about to switch it off when he stiffened and
said, "Yes. Give it to me."

It was a voice from the Communications Room, and it
said, "Report just came in of a man's body found floating

in bay. Throat cut. Ambulance dispatched to pier at Tenth Street to pick up for morgue. Unidentified man in rowboat reported body."

The three men in Will Gentry's private office sat very silent for a long moment. Then Shayne asked quietly, "The Hibiscus fronts on the bay, doesn't it?"

"Right on the edge overlooking it," Rourke said.

Shayne got to his feet and the others followed suit. He said, "If either three-sixty or three-sixteen face the east—"

Gentry nodded. "I think it's time we took a look at the Hibiscus. We can go to the morgue from there."

They went out together, parting at the end of the corridor with Gentry going ahead for his own car, Rourke and Shayne turning out a side door to ride together in the detective's Hudson.

They made it to the Hibiscus in a few minutes, and as Shayne pulled into the curb in front, Gentry's automobile with two uniformed men in the front seat nosed in behind them.

The trio entered the hotel together, and Dick and the bell-captain snapped to attention when they recognized the bulky figure of Miami's Chief of Police.

Dick spoke hurriedly over his shoulder to Evelyn, and as they came up to the desk he said brightly, "Good evening. Do you want Mr. Patton? He'll be right out."

Gentry nodded. He asked, "What third-floor rooms front on the bay? Either three-sixty or three-sixteen?"

"Why, three-sixteen does, Chief. Three-sixty is—"

Gentry nodded, a pleased look on his face. He turned from the desk as the house detective came wheezing around the corner toward them. He said, "Evening, Ollie," shaking hands briefly. "You know Shayne and Tim Rourke, don't you?"

"Sure." Patton nodded at the reporter and detective. "Tried to call you a short time ago, Mike. You know, you asked me to keep in touch if anything more came up on the Paulsons?"

"Yeh. What?"

"Her brother was in here asking for her. Big guy with a scar on his face. Just drove in from Jacksonville, he claimed, and she was supposed to be expecting him and he wanted to wait up in her room for her. Funny thing was, he decided he didn't want to wait when I offered to go up and sit it out with him. In fact, he made a funny excuse to beat it—saying he'd be back."

Gentry said, "Interesting. Let's go up and have a look at this room where you keep your bodies hidden, Ollie."

As they went to the elevator in a solid group, Patton said forlornly, "Hope you don't think I was negligent about not reporting all this crazy stuff, Chief. As a matter of fact, we're not even sure which room the body was supposed to be in. And then when there wasn't any body at all—"

Shayne said flatly, "It was three-sixteen, Oliver. Miss Paulson explained to me about the mix-up in room numbers. After seeing her brother's body in three-sixteen, she rushed out to find another phone to report it on. Three-sixty was conveniently open and she used the phone in there. When she got back a few minutes later, the body had disappeared."

"Her brother's body?" Patton asked in puzzlement as they went up. "But I've just been telling you he was here looking for her."

"Not her brother," Gentry said. "We got a description of him from Jax."

"He had plenty of identification," Patton protested. "I made him show it when he wanted in to her room."

The elevator stopped and they got out. Shayne said, "Yeh. He showed me his identification, too."

As Patton led the way down the dim-lit corridor, he said thoughtfully, "Maybe that begins to add up then. Though

the guy said he just got in from Jacksonville, the elevator
boy swears he's been around before. Either earlier in the
evening or the last day or so."

"Yeh, it adds up," Shayne agreed. "He was here about
nine-thirty. Just when the body was doing its disappearing
act."

Patton had stopped in front of 316 and he knocked per-
functorily before fitting a key in the lock. He opened the
door and reached inside to turn on the overhead light,
then stepped back. "There it is," he muttered defensively.
"See if you can find a body."

The three entered and stood staring at the smoothly
made-up bed standing directly beneath two closed windows. The only way to reach the windows to open or close
them was to get on the bed or move it from the wall. Gentry went to the rear and told Shayne, "Take the front and
let's move it out. None of you touch the bed. These windows closed when you looked in before, Ollie?"

"Yes. I remember noticing because it was hot. Most
guests keep them open all the time."

Gentry grunted as he and Shayne moved the bed two
feet nearer the center of the room. He and Shayne circled
from opposite ends of the bed and stood side by side studying the windows without touching them. Through the
panes, they could see the riding lights of half a dozen
yachts in the Municipal Basin not far distant. They were
ordinary sash windows that could be raised or lowered,
and they weren't latched. There were outside screens with
hooks and eyes to hold them shut. Both screens were
hooked now, but without closer examination it would be
impossible to know whether either had been unhooked
recently or not.

Looking downward as directly as they could without
opening the windows, they could see tiny whitecaps rolling
in from the bay, and could hear them breaking lightly on
the stone wall directly below.

Gentry stepped back with a shrug, saying, "Nobody touch anything. I want this room kept locked, Ollie, until my boys go over it. Did you touch anything at all when you were first up here? Smooth the bed or anything?"

"Nothing, Will. I just looked in the bathroom and closet and peeked under the bed to make sure there weren't any corpses."

"Water directly below these windows?" pursued Gentry. "No strip of sand to catch a body if it were shoved out?"

"Only at low tide. There's about ten feet of sand then. It was high tide about nine tonight. Going down now."

Will Gentry nodded, moving toward the open door. "About all we can do here. Lock the door, Ollie. I'll send a man up to guard it until the Identification Squad gets here. And for your information, there's an All Cars out on both Nellie Paulson and the lad with the scar who's carrying her brother's wallet around with him. I'll put a couple of men downstairs in case either of them show."

"Sure. Whatever you say, Chief. Uh—you got reason to believe a man was killed in this room tonight? His body shoved out the window into the bay?"

"Right now, it's a good bet," said Gentry placidly. "I'm not blaming you for anything—yet. Just keep your nose clean and for God's sake don't try to cover up if anything else funny happens. Your job's one thing, but accessory-after-the-fact is something else again."

Outside the hotel, Tim Rourke and Shayne got into Shayne's car while Gentry sent one of his men up to watch outside 316 and called headquarters over the two-way radio in the police car.

Shayne pulled away slowly, and Rourke slouched down beside him and lit a cigarette, speaking for the first time since they entered the hotel:

"What do you make of it now?"

Hunched over the wheel, Shayne growled, "Let's take a look at what's waiting for us in the morgue before we do any more guessing. You know every damn bit as much about all of it as I do. I didn't hold out anything on Will."

"Only difference is—you talked to the girl personally and we didn't. If she isn't nuts—"

"Doesn't it begin to look more and more as though she isn't?" demanded Shayne. "It sounded hay-wire at first when she claimed she'd seen her dead brother and then scar-face claimed *he* was her brother. Now we know he isn't. And with this body picked up in the bay, there's a hell of a good chance we'll discover he was in three-sixteen just as she said, and was shoved out the window while she was looking for a phone."

"By scar-face?"

"It looks reasonable. Hell!" said Shayne with irritation, "I don't know. If he is the murderer and knows she's the only one who's actually seen the body in three-sixteen, it would give him a good motive for tracing her to my place and then trying so desperately first to make me think she's nuts and then to get his hands on her. Without her to testify about her brother's body, the corpse might well have drifted out to sea and never been found—or, at least, not until it was unrecognizable."

"Yeh. And it would explain how he came by Bert Paulson's wallet. If he killed the guy. But what's the Roney Plaza angle she handed you? Why didn't she tell you she was staying at the Hibiscus?"

"That's one of several things," said Shayne wearily, "that I want to ask her the next time she and I have a tête-à-tête."

He slowed his car as he approached a building with stone steps leading up from the sidewalk, twin lights burning at the top.

Will Gentry's official car wasn't in sight as they went up the steps to the morgue entrance.

The night attendant was a wizened man with a wide gap in his front teeth that showed when he grinned at the detective and reporter from behind a scarred desk with a bright light overhead. Doctor Martin, the police surgeon, stood beside the desk as they entered, and he frowned, looking past them.

"Where's Will? I understood he was in on this personally."

Shayne said, "He'll be along. You looked over the stiff they pulled out of the bay, Doc?"

Martin nodded. "Not much to look at."

"Throat cut?"

"Like a stuck pig." The doctor made a slashing motion with the side of his hand from left to right.

"Any identification?"

"Plenty. Bill-fold in his hip pocket with cards and stuff. No money."

The doctor looked past Shayne as another car stopped in front. A door slammed and solid footsteps sounded on the stone steps. Will Gentry came in heavily, nodding to the police doctor and attendant. "Been over him, Doc?"

"Superficially. Throat cut all the way across with a very sharp knife or razor. One to two hours ago. I'd say he went in the water quite soon after death."

"Lots of blood?" asked Gentry matter-of-factly.

"Lots."

"What Will wonders," said Shayne, "is whether the job could have been done in a hotel room, say, without leaving any traces of blood behind if he were shoved out a window fast."

Martin's eyes were bright with speculation. "It would have spurted," he said doubtfully. "If a pillow or blanket had been held ready and shoved over the wound fast, it might have soaked up the blood without leaving any around. That what you mean?"

"Or a man's coat?" Shayne asked sharply.

"Yes. A man's coat." Martin shrugged. "He's wearing no coat, by the way. In his shirt-sleeves."

"Identification?" asked Gentry.

The attendant opened a desk drawer and drew out a manilla envelope. He handed it to the chief who tore it open and withdrew an obviously expensive sealskin billfold that was still heavy with water. There were two credit identification cards from well-known hotels in New York, an accident insurance identification card.

All gave the name of Charles Barnes, and the insurance card gave an address on East 63rd Street, New York City.

"That's everything we found on him," said Martin. "Not even a buck in the wallet. He's young. Twenty to twenty-five. Healthy. No distinguishing marks. Five-ten or eleven, at a guess. Around a hundred and fifty before the blood drained out of him. You want anything else from me tonight, Will?"

"What's that?" said Gentry absently. "Five-ten and a hundred-fifty, huh? I guess not, Doc. Unless something comes up. That remind you of anything, Mike?"

"Nothing except the description we had from the Jacksonville police tonight on Bert Paulson." Shayne's gray eyes were very bright. "Let's go down for a look."

The attendant got up hastily and preceded the three men to a heavy door in the rear opening onto a flight of stairs leading down into the concrete-lined coldroom. A dank chillness came up the stairs to meet them as they started down. Though air-conditioned, the square room seemed to hold an indefinable odor of all the corpses that had been stored there for varying lengths of time over the years.

There were two white enamel tables under a glaring light in the center of the room, a bank of white, over-sized filing cabinets along one wall. Each cabinet had three drawers about six feet long and three feet square.

The attendant went to the lower drawer at one end, and pulled it out its full length on ball-bearing rollers. He flipped back a white sheet to show the naked body lying on its back in the drawer.

The face was chalk-white, paler by far than any dead person Shayne had ever seen before. The eyes were closed, mouth sagging open in a macabre sort of grin. The features were even, and had probably been handsome when the young man was alive. There was a wide, gaping wound in his throat, edges of the flesh cut cleanly as though at one stroke, shriveled now by exposure to bay water.

The three men stood together, silently looking down at the corpse. Gentry said heavily, "Charles Barnes from New York? I wonder."

"Yeh," said Rourke quickly. "Why not Bert Paulson from Jacksonville? Description fits. It all adds up to the girl's story. If scar-face slit his throat and switched wallets —there's your complete explanation, Mike. So she did see her brother lying there murdered. Didn't you say she told you his coat was folded up under his head? It could have been used to staunch the blood as you suggested upstairs."

Shayne didn't reply. His eyes were narrowed and very bright behind slitted lids as he stared down at the dead man. His left hand went up absently to tug at the lobe of his ear.

He had a disquieting sense of recognition as he stood there. It had hit him hard but fleetingly at first glance. It went away when he strove to pin it down in his mind, but the feeling remained, elusive and tantalizing.

Without taking his gaze from the white face, he muttered, "I've seen him some place. Recently. I swear it." He closed his eyes tightly and his rugged features hardened in a mask of concentration.

Gentry and Rourke waited without speaking. He shook his head slowly, still not opening his eyes. He muttered, "It runs away from me. Like quicksilver. I know I've seen him. Probably just once and briefly. It isn't real familiarity. But

it's there. Just beyond my goddamned conscious grasp of
it."

He opened his eyes suddenly for another long look at the
pallid face. He shook his head disgustedly and turned
away. "I have to put it out of my mind. It'll pop up unexpectedly. I *know* I should recognize him, and I know it's
important. 'Way down deep beyond reason, something
tells me it's damned important. That we'll know some
answers when it comes back to me."

The others turned away behind him and the attendant
closed the drawer with a soft thud.

Shayne had reached the stairway and started up when
he whirled about abruptly, his face lighting with satis-
faction. "Got it! And it messes up our nice little theory all
to hell. That guy couldn't possibly have been murdered
in the Hibiscus Hotel at nine-thirty tonight. At ten
o'clock he was alive in the Silver Glade."

He was fumbling in the side pocket of his jacket, and
he pulled out the photo the girl had thrust into it in the
lobby of his hotel while she was importuning him to accept a retainer from her.

He thrust the photograph at Will Gentry. "Take it back
and compare the two. You'll see it's the same man."

FOURTEEN: *11:12 P.M.*

Michael Shayne dropped Timothy Rourke at the *News* Tower on his way back from the morgue to police headquarters. The reporter was anxious to get out a preliminary story on the "Body in the Bay" as he was already calling it in headlines, and he promised Shayne to withhold most of the other stuff the detective had given him, merely mentioning the curious incident that had happened at a local hotel earlier, without naming the Hibiscus and without using the Paulson name in connection with the dead man.

Back in Will Gentry's office at headquarters, Shayne found the chief about to interrogate a quiet-faced bronzed man who was clad only in skin-tight swimming trunks and whom Gentry introduced as Norman Raine.

"Mr. Raine brought the body in from the bay," he told Shayne. "I've got wires out to New York and to Jacksonville. Let's hear what Mr. Raine has to tell us."

"It isn't much and I'm afraid it won't be very helpful," Raine said in a resonant baritone. "I've a boat anchored in the yacht basin and I sleep aboard—alone. Only tonight I couldn't sleep." He showed even, white teeth in a smile and nodded thankfully as he leaned forward to accept a cigarette from the redhead, averting his eyes from the black cigar Gentry puffed on.

He drew in smoke and expelled it, leaned back comfortably and went on, "That's what brought me ashore in my skiff. I was out of cigarettes, and about ten-thirty I got to the point where I just had to have a smoke. So I started rowing in."

"You're anchored off Tenth Street?" asked Gentry.

"Just about opposite the end of Tenth. The tide was running out, but there was a nice breeze behind me and I was pulling along steadily, about half-way to shore I guess, when suddenly my bow struck something in the water.

"It gave me quite a start. It was a funny, solid, dead sort of thud. You know, I was rowing along thinking about nothing at all except about a cigarette and how good the first puff was going to taste, and then—pow! Like that.

"Well, the poor devil was floating face down in the water. I saw he must be a goner right away. Face down and all. I had a little trouble getting him aboard, and then went on in as fast as I could. I tied up and ran to the nearest place I saw a light, and telephoned the police. That's absolutely all I know about it."

"How far out are you anchored?" Shayne asked him.

"About—oh—a half mile. It's the *Marjie J*. You can check it easily enough. She's a forty-foot single-master."

"Then you'd say you were about a quarter mile off-shore when you struck the body?"

"Something like that. It's purely a guess, of course, but the best I can do under the circumstances."

Will Gentry removed his cigar from between his teeth and nodded. "Anything else occur to you, Mike?"

Shayne shook his head. "I don't see how Mr. Raine can help us any more than that. You didn't search the body?" he added.

"Naturally not." Raine was quite properly indignant. "I could see it was murder right away and I didn't touch him."

Gentry got up to shake his hand. "Thanks for being so co-operative, Mr. Raine. You're not pulling out right away?"

"Not for ten days at least."

"A man outside will drive you back to the pier," Gentry told him. "Have him stop some place for you to buy cigarettes." He shrugged when the door closed behind the man. "Without getting technical with tide and current tables, I'd say it matches up with the Hibiscus pretty well."

"I know." Shayne scowled angrily. "But you can't get away from the gal who tried to force a hundred and forty bucks on me at ten o'clock to pick the guy up at the Silver Glade."

"I'm not trying to get away from her. Maybe she was mistaken. Maybe she just thought he was there at that time. Maybe she was lying like hell."

"Why?"

"I don't know why. Why does any woman lie?"

"If I'd taken the assignment, I was bound to find out at once that he wasn't there," Shayne pointed out.

"But you didn't take it. I wish to God you had. Then we wouldn't have all these other unanswered questions."

"Any report from your boys at the Hibiscus yet?"

"I'm waiting for it." Gentry drummed fingertips on his desk irritably. "There's a telephone listed for Barnes at that New York address. It didn't answer. I phoned the police to get anything they could on Barnes. And I've got a detective driving down from Jax with a picture of Bert and Nellie Paulson. Nothing to do but mark time, I guess."

Shayne squirmed uncomfortably in his chair. He wished, now, that he had told Gentry in the beginning about sending the girl to Lucy's apartment. He wasn't quite sure why he had held that fact out. With a vague feeling of protecting her, he supposed glumly. In a sense, he looked on her as a client, and until he knew more about the case he had instinctively withheld the information that would have automatically brought her in for police interrogation.

Now he probably had a positive identification of the dead man in the palm of his hand, but he hesitated to admit that fact to Will Gentry yet. The chief would be

sore as a boil because Shayne hadn't told him earlier, and
Shayne still felt there were a lot of things he'd like to know
about the case before seeking a showdown with her.

Of course, if she were just a cheap little accomplice in
a badger racket in which her brother had gotten himself
murdered, he had no sympathy for her at all. But he
couldn't help feeling there was something mixed-up in
that diagnosis. Recalling her as he had first seen her waiting for him in his room, she simply didn't fit into the picture that way.

He was roused from his brief reverie by a tap on the
door and the entrance of Sergeant Hopkins of the Identification Squad.

He was young and square-jawed and had a crew-cut, and
was not in uniform. He nodded incuriously to Shayne,
stood stiffly in front of the desk and reported, "I'm just
back from the Hibiscus, sir. We gave three-sixteen the
works."

"Well?" Gentry rumbled.

"We got nothing very definite, I'm afraid. Photographs
of the bed with careful lighting indicates someone has
lain heavily on it since it was made up. We found no blood-
stains. One set of fingerprints pretty well all over, in
places that indicate they must be from the occupant of
the room—another set that we checked out as the hotel
maid. Prints of an unidentified man on the door-frame
and the back of a chair."

When he stopped, Shayne broke in, "What about the
windows?"

The sergeant regarded him stolidly. "Only the occupant's prints there. One of the screens is very tightly
latched and probably hasn't been opened for months. The
other opens easily and there was no dust underneath or
on the sill." He shrugged and added, "On the other hand,
the maid says she quite likely opened it herself recently
in cleaning up the room. She can't swear to that, so there's

nothing conclusive either way. It certainly could have been opened tonight to allow a body to be shoved out, but there's no way of proving that happened."

Gentry took his saliva-soaked half cigar from his mouth and glared at it, fielded it expertly into the spittoon. "Get out to the morgue and fingerprint the Barnes stiff. See if they check with the extra set you found in the room and let me know."

He shrugged at Shayne as the young sergeant wheeled about and went out. "Wouldn't you know that's about what we'd get?" he demanded savagely.

Shayne let out a deep sigh. "I guess that puts it straight up to me."

"Puts what up to you?"

"You're not going to like it, Will."

"Holding out on me?" Gentry was instantly and suspiciously alert.

"Not very much, but— I guess we'd better see if we can get our corpse identified before we do any more guessing."

"It wouldn't be a bad idea at all," Gentry agreed in a very smooth voice. "You got an idea?"

Shayne grinned at him. "The girl who claims he's her brother."

Gentry's heavy black brows came down threateningly. "You told me she ran out on you. Down your fire escape and disappeared."

"She did. But I somehow forgot to mention that before she went into the kitchen I'd given her Lucy's address with a note to Lucy, and told her to go there."

"Goddamn it, Mike! Do you mean to say you've got reason to think she's at Lucy's now?"

Shayne kept his grin working and said lightly, "I can do better than that. I know she is. Remember when Lucy telephoned? That was to say she'd arrived safely."

Shayne reached for the telephone hastily as a rumble of anger spilled out from between Gentry's thick lips.

"You've got to admit we're lucky to have her on tap this way." He gave Lucy's number into the phone and settled back, not looking at Gentry who was cursing in low monosyllables.

He listened to her phone ring five times before she answered. Then her voice sounded curiously thick, and the words were fuzzy at the edges. "Hello. Who is this?"

"Mike. Have you been asleep?"

"Just dozed off, I guess."

"Well, get yourself waked up," he said impatiently. "Both of you. I'm on my way over."

"Both of us? What do you mean, Michael?"

"Miss Paulson. Is she in bed?"

"But she left, Michael."

"What? When? Goddamn it, Lucy, I sent her there for you to take care of her."

"You didn't tell me I was to lock her in, did you? How was I to keep her here if she decided not to stay?"

"When did she leave, Lucy? What did she say?"

"Fifteen or twenty minutes ago. She didn't say anything. Just thank you for the drink and I tank I go home now. And she went."

Shayne slammed the phone down to prevent himself from taking any more of his sickening anger out on Lucy. He looked up, bracing himself to meet Gentry's fierce gaze, and said unnecessarily:

"She's ducked out on us, Will. God knows where—or why."

FIFTEEN: *11:20 P.M.*

As Lucy Hamilton put the telephone down in her apartment, she sat silently and with bowed head for a long moment, feeling the impact of her employer's anger and sensing his frustrated disappointment in her as he slammed down at his end.

The only sound in the apartment was the labored breathing of her guest standing close behind her.

Lucy fought to remain calm, lifting her head finally and forcing herself to turn and ask listlessly, "Is that what you wanted me to do?"

"You were just fine that time. If he calls back again, or anyone else, be damn sure and tell them not to come here tonight. That you're in bed or sick or something—or else you get *this* fast."

Lucy shuddered and closed her eyes as the ugly, short-bladed knife made a sickening arc close to her throat. She heard a pleased giggle bubble up out of the other girl's throat. There was already blood on the blade of that knife. Whose, she didn't know. The girl hadn't said whose blood it was as she calmly withdrew it from her bag and displayed it when Shayne's call came through.

But the fierce glitter in her eyes as she crisply told Lucy what to say over the phone had been proof enough that she wouldn't hesitate to use the knife again if she were thwarted in any way.

It was all so utterly incomprehensible. They had been sitting on the sofa calmly chatting away when the phone rang and Lucy had involuntarily exclaimed, "That'll be

Michael now." The other girl had been telling her an involved story about being in Shayne's apartment when some man had come looking for her and how she'd escaped down the fire escape.

Then the wild gleam in the girl's eyes and the blood-stained knife that came leaping out of the suede bag!

Now the girl backed away from her and said calmly, "Get up and move away from the telephone. You won't get hurt if you do exactly as I say. Not until I can fix things up a little better anyhow. Then we'll see. Sit in that chair across the room and don't move out of it while I use the phone."

Lucy stood up slowly, averting her gaze from the knife. She crossed to the indicated chair and sat down. She heard the girl dialing, and tried to concentrate on the clicking of the dial to try and get the number—although Shayne had often laughed at fictional detectives who were supposed to be able to accomplish that trick.

She heard the girl ask, "Is Mr. Bert Paulson there?" and say after a moment, "If he does come in soon, please give him this message. It's very important. He's to call his sister at this number." And she read Lucy's number from the telephone.

Then she hung up and sat quietly for a moment, biting her under-lip broodingly and frowning across the room with eyes that seemed not quite to focus.

She nodded her blonde head slowly after thinking for a moment, dialed another number and repeated exactly the same instructions she had given on the first call.

After hanging up the second time, she got up from the chair and moved back a few feet, gesturing to Lucy with her knife. "Sit down here by the phone and do exactly as I tell you if you ever want to see your precious Michael Shayne again. Wait a minute though," she said rapidly as Lucy dragged herself up. "Go into the bedroom first and get a sheet and bring it out. I'll be right behind you all the time."

Lucy went into the bedroom and got a sheet from her linen closet. Her mind was working desperately to think of some ruse to escape or overcome her visitor, but even years of close association with Michael Shayne had not fitted her to cope with exactly this situation. She was bitterly certain he could think of all sorts of clever things to do under the same circumstances, but why, oh! *why,* had he sent this insanc girl to take refuge in her apartment with a bloody knife in her handbag?

"Drop the sheet on the floor," she was directed, "and then sit in that chair beside the telephone. If any calls come, you'll have to answer them in case it isn't Lanny calling for me. And everything will be a lot easier if I just tie you up so you won't get any funny ideas. Don't think *I* care whether you keep on living or not," the voice went on coldly as the girl picked up the sheet and slit strips in it which she ripped all the way across.

"It's just that you're my insurance, see? I've *got* to get that call from Lanny, and I figure this is just about the safest place to stay until it comes." She giggled happily again as she came up behind Lucy with three long strips of sheeting trailing behind her.

"Who'd think of looking for me holed up cozily with the great detective's girl-friend? Put your feet back solid against the legs of the chair. And lay your right forearm on the arm of it. I'll leave your left hand free to manage the phone."

Lucy sat tense and strained in the chair, biting her under-lip hard as the other knelt beside her and started winding a strip of cloth around each ankle and the chairlegs.

Now? Was this the moment? If she twisted quickly and tried to throw herself and the chair on top of the girl?

No. Her instinct for self-preservation was too strong. *Some*thing would happen. Something would have to happen. Michael would certainly come. He had sounded so terribly outraged and angry when she told him the girl had already left. Certainly he would be arriving in a few minutes to question her more closely.

It had all happened so fast. She'd had no chance to adjust her thoughts and think of something to say over the telephone that would indicate to him that she was talking under duress. But she had tried desperately to be flip about it and not even apologize for letting the girl go. That should be a clue he would understand.

But suppose he didn't? Suppose he thought she was just being jealous and irritated because he had gone off at the summons of an unknown blonde instead of staying with her? She hadn't tried to conceal her feelings earlier when he had dashed off, leaving his drink untouched behind him.

Now her legs and right arm were bound tightly to the chair and she was helpless. It was too late now to make any attempt. If Michael would only come or telephone again! She began thinking desperately of something she might say to him if he did call that would not arouse the girl's suspicions but would tell *him* what she wanted to convey.

Her captor stepped back coolly to survey her work, and she nodded with a smile that held more venom than humor. She walked across to the sofa to drop the knife into her open bag and sat down, saying, "Now we're real comfy. Just so you don't try to say the wrong thing over the phone if it rings. If it's someone asking for Nellie or Miss Paulson, just say I'm here and I'll take it from there. But if it's anyone else, you be damn careful to stall them off. No matter what you scream over the phone or how fast they can get here—it'll be too late to do you any good." She leaned forward to pick up her drink, and smacked her lips with relish as she sipped it.

"I just don't understand," faltered Lucy. "Why did Michael send you here? Why did you *come* when—when—?"

"When the police are looking for me for murder?" The question came equably and with frightening calm. "You are perfectly right, darling. That is blood you saw on my little knife." The words came out purringly with hidden, deadly menace. It rose suddenly on a note of shrill derision:

"Because he's a fool. Like any man I ever met, he falls all over himself for a smile and a sad story any girl wants to dish out. And by God, how I love to make suckers out of them. I'll tell you all about it because, you know, you're never going to repeat a word of it to anyone. I promise you that. Just something for you to think about, dearie, while I'm waiting for that phone call."

Lucy sat straining stiffly against her bonds. Get her talking! That was it. Keep her boasting and talking about what she had done. She might finally get hysterical and blow her top completely.

"I want to get it absolutely straight about the telephone call you're expecting," she said as placatingly as she could. "So I won't make any bobbles that'll get you mad at me. Is it someone named Lanny whom you expect to call?"

"That's what I said, isn't it?"

"But when you made your calls I heard you ask for someone named Bert Paulson. And leave word for him to call his sister here. But if it's really someone named Lanny you want, will *he* ask for his sister if he calls?"

"Never mind about whose sister I am or anything." The girl on the sofa turned sullen. "Just you do what I said about answering the phone. If it's Lanny and if he asks for his sister or Nellie, or— Well, if he just says it's Lanny, you give it to me quick."

She fumbled in her bag, took out the knife and studied it fondly. Then, unexpectedly, she giggled. "Oh shucks, why don't I tell you who I really am, and Lanny and all? Just show you how dumb your silly Michael Shayne really is. Take this note he wrote to you to begin with—"

"By God!" said Will Gentry violently as Shayne reported what Lucy had said on the phone. "By God, Mike. So that's the way you protect your client. Turn her loose to go out on the town and keep a tryst with a killer gunning for her with a forty-five?"

"How was I to know she wouldn't stay put once she was safe with Lucy? As for keeping any trysts with a forty-five—I'm damn sure that isn't why she went out. If you'd seen how frightened she was of meeting him at my place—"

"Playing God again." Chief Gentry's fist thudded down angrily on his desk. "If you'd come clean with me in the beginning, she'd be safe right now. You know that, don't you?"

"Sure, but—"

"But, hell!" raged the police chief. "You never change, do you, Mike? You've got some kind of goddamned God-complex that makes you pull things like this. High-and-mighty Michael Shayne sitting back and pulling the strings. Manipulating people like puppets to make 'em jump the way *he* thinks they ought to jump. If for once in your life you'd come down to earth and co-operate with the police, things would be one hell of a lot better for everybody concerned."

"All right," said Shayne grimly. "So hind-sight says you're right. But things are no worse off right now than you thought they were ten minutes ago before I told you I had her stashed at Lucy's. You've got a pick-up on both of them. Chances are you'll have them both before he can get to her."

"But it won't be your doing if that's the way it happens. Goddamn it, Mike—"

"This isn't getting us anywhere," interposed Shayne. "You can sit here on your dead butt and rave all you want to, but we'll still be going around in circles in the dark. Let's take this systematically. From what we know now, do you believe the dead man was seen by Nellie Paulson in the Hibiscus at nine-thirty and then shoved out the window into the bay?"

Gentry had another cigar out and was chewing on it savagely without lighting it. "That's my guess. Even if some dame did try to place him alive in the Silver Glade at ten."

"All right. Taking that for a starter. Are you assuming that my scar-faced friend is actually Charles Barnes from New York, that the dead man is Bert Paulson as his sister insisted—and that Barnes switched identification after killing Paulson in his sister's room?"

"How else do you read it?"

Shayne shrugged. "I'm just looking at all the possibilities. I guess we might assume Barnes was slated to be the next sucker in the Paulsons' brother-and-sister act, and he objected with a sharp knife. That the way you see it?"

"It's all theorizing at this point," grunted Gentry. "Without any solid facts to go on—"

"But all we can do right now is theorize. I keep going back to what Nellie Paulson told me in my room. Why did she claim she and her brother were staying at the Roney when we know she'd had that room at the Hibiscus for two weeks? And where's her brother been staying these two weeks?"

"You tell me. You're so damned pat with the answers."

Shayne tugged at his ear-lobe and frowned. "If Barnes is the killer, it would explain why he was so anxious to get his hands on Nellie—why he pretended to me he was her brother so I'd hand her over to him—and why he hurried back to the Hibiscus and tried to contact her there, still playing the brother angle."

"Because she's the only one who's actually seen the body," agreed Gentry gruffly. "The only person alive who can testify there was a body in three-sixteen tonight. Sure. That makes sense. But how do you add in the other girl who tried to finger a dead man as being alive in the Silver Glade half an hour after he'd been dumped in the bay? Who the hell is she and how does she come into this?"

Shayne said, "She's the one piece that doesn't fit into our pat little theory." He shook his head irritably, running his hand through bristly red hair. "Yet she's got to fit. She's the key-piece right now. It wasn't coincidence that put her in my hotel with that picture at ten o'clock."

"Find her then," grunted Gentry. "Find her among the few hundred thousand people in Miami, and let's ask her. For God's sake, Mike, you didn't even take the trouble to ask her name when she was right there in front of you. Hell of a way to play detective."

"I didn't know she fitted into the picture. Hell! At that point, I didn't know there *was* any picture for her to fit into. Remember, that was before I'd even talked to Nellie. I took her for another jealous wife trying to pin down some divorce evidence."

"Maybe she is at that. Maybe Paulson is married—or was—and she's the wife—or widow, now."

Shayne shook his head stubbornly. "Then what made her think he was in the Silver Glade when we know he was more likely floating in the bay at that moment?"

"None of these questions are any good at this point," snapped Gentry. "Maybe she'd made a date earlier in the night to meet him there and just assumed that's where he was. And maybe *she* killed him and was trying to give herself an alibi by playing you for a sucker, expecting you to come along later just as you did and swear the guy was still alive at ten o'clock. To hell with all this," Gentry ended flatly. "Get out and hunt up some answers to the questions you've been asking. You know both of them by sight. That's more than any of my men have got. You messed everything up by playing it smart and letting the girl get away from Lucy. Get out in Miami and find her before she ends up with her throat cut or a forty-five slug in her belly."

"Yeh," said Shayne, "I guess you're right. It is my baby now." He pushed back his chair and stood up, rubbing his angular jaw thoughtfully. "I'll be calling in, huh? You ought to have a fingerprint report on the corpse soon. And New York might have something interesting to tell us about Barnes. How soon will the Jacksonville dick get here with pictures of the Paulsons?"

Will Gentry looked at the big electric clock on the wall behind him. "Any time now. Good hunting, Mike. But goddamn it, if you'd just—"

Shayne said grimly, "I know. Don't rub it in. If anything happens to that girl now, it'll be bad enough without you rubbing my face in it."

His wide shoulders slumped a little, and he turned and slouched out of Gentry's office.

SEVENTEEN: *11:27 P.M.*

There was an air of elegance, a feeling of almost oppressive luxury about the huge lobby of the Roney Plaza Hotel on Miami Beach. At this hour of night and before the winter season had officially opened, the lobby was none-the-less quite well filled with gay couples in evening dress, coming and going from the bank of elevators to the cocktail and dining rooms where late supper was being served and dancing was in progress.

Michael Shayne made his way among the milling guests to the wide expanse of desk where two clerks were still on duty. He waited behind a fat man wearing a scarlet cummerbund and white jacket with midnight blue evening trousers, who was complaining bitterly to the clerk about the length of time it had taken room service to deliver two rye highballs to his suite earlier in the evening.

The clerk was a tall, lean, middle-aged man with a very thin black mustache and a pained expression of solicitude on his face as he listened patiently to the complaint. He agreed soothingly that it was a shocking state of affairs when a guest at the Roney had to wait more than fifteen minutes for delivery of a drink, and gravely promised to give the matter his personal attention and see that the offending waiter was reprimanded harshly. He then turned his tired eyes on Shayne and lifted his upper lip a quarter of an inch in what was supposed to pass for a smile, and inquired, "And what can I do for you, sir?"

"Do you have a Barnes registered? Charles Barnes from New York."

"If you'd care to inquire at the house telephone, sir?" The clerk flipped a white hand toward a row of phones at Shayne's right.

The detective started to protest but, realizing he'd get faster results by observing protocol, went to one of the phones and asked the same question.

A pleasant female voice repeated the name and said almost immediately, "Twelve-ten. Would you like me to ring them?"

Shayne said, "Please." He let the phone ring six times before replacing it.

He returned to the desk and said, "Barnes in twelve-ten? Can you tell me anything about him?"

The eyebrow-like mustache lifted superciliously. "I'm sure I don't know. If the telephone doesn't answer—"

Again, Shayne hesitated, and again he turned away with a slight shrug. He stepped back from the desk and lit a cigarette, looking around the lobby carefully.

He spotted a youngish man wearing a double-breasted blue serge suit leaning negligently against one of the pillars and apparently completely disinterested in everything that was going on about him.

Shayne threaded his way to him and asked, "Is Jimmie Curtis still in charge of Security?"

The young man looked at him stonily for a moment, then his face relaxed in a pleased smile. "You're Mike Shayne, aren't you?"

"That's right. Jimmie around?"

"He's not here any longer. Hasn't been for months. Mr. Gerdon took his place."

"And where," asked Shayne, "can I find Mr. Gerdon?"

"I'll take you to his office." The young man detached himself from the pillar and to Shayne's faint surprise it remained standing. He led him beyond the desk into a corridor, around a corner and down another with closed office doors on both sides.

He stopped near the end at a door marked "Private," knocked and then opened the door. He stepped inside and said smartly, "Mr. Gerdon. This is Mr. Shayne from Miami."

Shayne followed him in to a large room with a very thick carpet on the floor. A totally bald man with sunken cheeks and slightly protruding eyes sat behind a highly polished mahogany desk.

He said, "Shayne?" and rose slowly as his bulging eyes studied the rangy detective from across the bay. He nodded and said, "All right, Rawson," and held a hand out to Shayne without noticeable cordiality.

"Heard a lot about you, of course. Is this social or business?"

"Business." Shayne sat in the chair he indicated. "A man named Barnes in twelve-ten."

"No trouble, I hope." Gerdon turned in his swivel chair to a card filing cabinet and drew out a long drawer. He flipped through the cards and withdrew one, placed it on the desk in front of him.

Shayne said, "I'll know better when you give me the dope."

"Mr. and Miss Barnes from New York. Brother and sister. Twelve-ten is a two-bedroom suite," Gerdon explained. He read the New York address on East 63rd Street. "Credit rating A-1. They checked in sixteen days ago. Everything regular. Paid the first week's bill with a New York check that cleared." He looked up with a frown.

"What are their first names?"

"Charles and Mary."

Shayne leaned back in his chair and blew smoke at the ceiling. "Nothing else on their card, huh?"

"No notations of any sort. That means run-of-the-mill so far as any observations go."

Shayne said, "Can you get someone in who can describe them both to me?"

Gerdon hesitated. "If you'd tell me what you have in mind—?"

Shayne said, "A man carrying Charles Barnes's wallet was pulled out of the bay tonight. Dead. First time I knew he had a sister." His gaze was withdrawn, his voice speculative.

Gerdon sucked in his lips. He pressed a button on his desk, leaned forward to speak in a low tone into a small microphone on a stand in front of him on the polished mahogany. Then he leaned back and said, "We'll have the room-maid in. And the night-boy who serves that floor. Dead, eh? An accident?"

Shayne shook his head. "Murder." He moved the side of his hand across his throat expressively. "There's some question about the identity of the body—whether Barnes is dead or may have done the job himself. Would you work on the desk and switchboard? Try to find out about their movements tonight. Phone calls in or out?"

Gerdon's face indicated polite disbelief that any guest of the Roney Plaza could possibly be mixed up in anything as sordid as being a murderer or the victim of one.

However, he spoke into the microphone again at some length, and settled back as there was a light tap on his door. He called, "Come," and a pretty, plump girl dressed in a maid's uniform entered hesitantly. She looked quickly from Shayne to Gerdon, and then moved to stand in front of the desk with downcast eyes.

Gerdon glanced at a notation he had made and said, "It's all right, Irma. This gentleman would like to ask you a few questions about twelve-ten."

"That's Mr. Barnes and Miss Mary," she said questioningly, turning to Shayne. "Real nice, both of them, I'm sure."

"I'm glad to hear that, Irma," Shayne reassured her.

"First, I wish you'd describe them to me the best you can."

"Miss Mary is real pretty. A little thing. Young-like. About twenty, I guess. She's got real blonde hair and—and, well, she's real nice. A lady. You know. She always says thank you. And tips me when she wants something extra. I do hope nothing's wrong."

Shayne said gravely, "I hope so too. Now, about her brother. Does he—have a scarred face?"

"Oh, no." Irma looked shocked by the question. "Real nice-looking he is, too. Some older than Miss Mary, I guess, but not really if you know what I mean."

"You're sure about the scar?"

"Of course I'm sure. I've seen him plenty, being in and out like I am."

Shayne sighed. "About how tall? What weight?"

"Just medium, I'd say. Shorter than you by inches. I don't know how much men weigh. But he isn't fat—nor thin either. Just medium-like."

Shayne didn't show his disappointment. He said, "I know you're a smart girl, Irma, and you girls are trained to notice all sorts of things about your guests. Now think hard and see if you can remember anything in particular about the Barnes. Anything you overheard or noticed."

"Well, they— I'd say they had plenty of money and were used to nice things. Their clothes and all. And they acted like they were having a good time. Miss Mary in particular, she loved swimming and went in twice most every day. Mr. Barnes went out more than she did. And he—well, he had a sort of way about him." She drooped her head and a slight color crept into her cheeks.

"What sort of way?" Shayne urged her.

"Well, it was just—it wasn't nothing, really." The girl spread out her hands and her blush deepened as she looked up at Shayne. "You get used to it, sort of, working in a hotel. He'd say things to me sometimes—and—and touch me. But always joking, it was," she added hastily. "I never thought it meant anything. But Miss Mary she got mad once or twice and told him it wasn't nice to say those things and he had ought to be ashamed of himself. But he'd just laugh it off and say I didn't mind, did I? And I'd tell him no, of course. And that's all."

"Did they entertain much? Seem to have many friends in Miami?"

"No, they didn't for a fact. Miss Mary, she'd stay in mostly in the evenings. Have her dinner served up there a lot, and then she'd read."

"While her brother was out?" Shayne supplied.

"Well, yes. He likes a good time, all right. But that's why folks come to Miami on vacation, isn't it?"

Shayne agreed it was, and after a few more questions he dismissed her with thanks. He shook his head wryly at Gerdon when she went out.

"There went a beautiful theory up in thin smoke. I'm beginning to think maybe it is Barnes who was murdered. The rather vague description fits him all right. We may have to ask her to come over to the morgue to look at him."

"Anything you want," Gerdon said. There was another knock at the door and a very thin pimply-faced college boy came in and stood stiffly at attention.

Yes, he took care of twelve-ten until midnight, and knew both the occupants by sight—the girl much better than her brother because she was mostly in and wanting service while he was on duty.

His descriptions of Mary and Charles Barnes coincided in all important details with the maid's. He guessed Charles was twenty-five and his sister maybe twenty-one or two. He put Charles at five-eleven and about a hundred sixty pounds. He was equally positive about the absence of any scar on his face. Sometimes he'd have a late call

close to midnight for a scotch and soda after Charles had
come in, but he never saw him drunk. Miss Mary always
had a double martini before dinner when it was served in
their suite, and very rarely a drink later. Then, only one.
She tipped well, but not excessively, and according to him
it was a pleasure to take care of twelve-ten in comparison
to some of the other people he had on his floor.

As he was leaving, a girl came in the office with two
sheets of paper that had typing on them.

Gerdon studied them in frowning silence for a time.
They were day-by-day notations of out-going calls from
twelve-ten, kept by the hotel for billing purposes, and
they disclosed little of real interest to Shayne except the
recurrence of calls to a certain number in Miami which
he recognized at once as the Hibiscus Hotel.

The first day or so after registration there had been a
spate of local calls to various numbers, and two long-dis-
tance to New York. Then the calls lessened to two or three
or four each day. Generally before noon, and only a few
in the evenings.

Shayne studied the list as Gerdon passed it to him, found
the first listing of the Hibiscus number almost a week after
they arrived. Then it appeared irregularly every day or so
afterward. The last time that number had been called
was 4:30 p.m. of that day.

There was also a scribbled notation from the desk to the
effect that both Mr. and Miss Barnes were now out, and it
was believed both of them had been away most of the evening.

And that was all Shayne was able to get from the Roney
Plaza about Charles and Mary Barnes.

Gerdon politely asked if he cared to go over the suite,
but Shayne declined the offer. He did suggest that a definite watch be kept for the return of either of the Barneses,
immediate notification of the Miami police and quiet sur-
veillance in that event.

He also asked for a tap on the telephone in the suite to trace all incoming calls and to gather as much information about the callers as possible.

Then he thanked Gerdon for his co-operation and hurried back to Miami.

EIGHTEEN: *11:35 P.M.*

Chief Gentry was seated at his desk listening intently to the telephone when Shayne burst into his office in long strides. The chief looked up with a frown, shaking his head to indicate he didn't want to be interrupted when Shayne appeared on the point of breaking in.

The detective dropped into a chair and lit a cigarette morosely while Gentry continued to listen, interjecting an occasional, "I see," and, "Yes, go on."

There was a smugly satisfied look on Gentry's florid face when he finally said, "Thank you very much. I'll let you know if there's anything else," and put the phone down.

"That was New York," he told Shayne. "They checked the Barnes address and found it's a penthouse apartment on 63rd. Charles Barnes lives there with his younger sister, Mary. They closed the place a couple of weeks ago and took off for a month's vacation in Miami. How do you like that?"

"Just fine," Shayne said unhappily, squinting at him through blue cigarette smoke.

"And the forwarding address they left for mail is the Roney Plaza Hotel on the Beach," Gentry went on impressively. "All we need now is to check with the Roney to see if Barnes has a scar on his cheek—and we'll begin to know where we stand."

He reached for the phone, but Shayne stopped him with a gesture. "I just came from the Roney. Charles Barnes has no scar. His description fits the dead man to a T."

"I'll be— *You* just came from the Roney? How come?"

"I thought it was an angle that might be worth checking," Shayne said wearily. "Remember, the girl told me she and her brother were staying at the Roney?"

"The Paulson girl? But we know she had room three-sixteen at the Hibiscus."

"If it *was* the Paulson girl. If it wasn't Mary Barnes all the time."

"Wait a minute. You told me—"

Shayne got up and began to pace the floor, his rugged features twisted in a mask of concentration.

"I told you that *he* said her name was Nellie Paulson. The man with the scar. She didn't give any name to me. I hadn't got around to that when he came busting in and she locked herself in the kitchen. Naturally, I believed him," groaned Shayne. "His story about chasing her down the back stairs of the Hibiscus coincided precisely with her story, so I accepted the name he gave her."

"But we know from the Jacksonville description of Paulson that he was lying about being Nellie Paulson's brother," barked Gentry. "Who the devil is he if he isn't Barnes?"

"He isn't Barnes," said Shayne flatly. "At least he isn't the man registered at the Roney as Barnes." He dropped into a chair and stretched his long legs out wearily.

"If the dead man is Barnes—and I'm beginning to think he is—then it looks as though the girl who talked to me must be his sister Mary. Don't you see how it hangs together? She said her brother had gotten tangled up with some broad while on this vacation. That he called her from the Hibiscus tonight to come and get him out of a jam. The records show several calls from the Barnes suite in the Roney to the Hibiscus in the past week. So what kind of jam does it look as though he might have been in?

"The old badger game, of course. With Miss Nellie Paulson of room three-sixteen in the Hibiscus. But some-

thing happens before Mary gets there to help him out. A
knife in his throat, no less. And Mary walks in before
they have time to get rid of the body. She takes one look
at her brother, and runs to use the phone in three-sixty.
By the time she gets back, his body has gone out the window. Then scar-face jumps her and she runs to me. And
then runs away from me when he follows her there."

"To Lucy's apartment," said Gentry sharply. "With a
note from you telling Lucy to look after her."

Shayne stared at him queerly and reached for the phone.
"I'll be damned if I know," he muttered, "whether Lucy
mentioned her by name to me or not. If it was Mary
Barnes instead of Nellie Paulson—"

He gave Lucy's number and waited. Again, the telephone rang several times before Lucy answered. And again
her voice sounded queerly strained when she said, "Yes?
What do you want?"

"Mike, angel. Listen carefully and think before you
reply. Did the girl who brought the note from me tell you
what her name was?"

"Why—you told me, Michael. When you called me on
the phone before she got here. Don't you remember? You
said Nellie Paulson would be along—"

"I *know* I did," he interrupted harshly. "But now I'm
asking you if she corroborated that."

"I—wait a minute. I'm trying to think. N-No. Not directly, I think. I just assumed from what you said that—
She did have a note from you."

"I know," said Shayne wearily. " 'Bye." He hung up
and told Gentry, "She didn't say anything to Lucy that
proves it either way. I'll be damned if I don't believe she
was Mary Barnes all along. I've had a feeling about her—
that she didn't fit into the badger game technique—"

"Then why did the scar-faced man positively identify
her as Nellie Paulson?"

"Don't forget that we now know he isn't Paulson,"

Shayne objected. "God knows who he is, but he doesn't fit the Jax police description. So maybe he didn't even know Nellie by sight. Maybe that's why he thought the girl who ran out of three-sixteen was Nellie. If he knew Nellie had that room—went up there looking for her and saw a blonde girl running out, he'd naturally assume she was Nellie. Now we're beginning to get somewhere."

"Where?" demanded Gentry sardonically.

"I don't know for sure." Shayne's grin was wryly abashed. "But the girl's story all falls into place if you accept her as Mary Barnes instead of Paulson. Damn it, I had a feeling from the beginning she was telling me the truth and wasn't half as crazy as Nellie Paulson is supposed to be."

"So now everything's just perfect—since you decided your judgment of her wasn't at fault."

"Everything's perfectly wrong," snapped Shayne. "I wasn't half as worried when I thought scar-face was hunting Nellie Paulson with a gun. Girls who pull stunts like her badger game pretty damn well deserve whatever they get. But if it's Mary Barnes he's after? Why the devil don't your men pick him up, Will? They've had his description for a couple of hours now."

"They will. Eventually. If he tries to move around. While you're blaming the Force, Mike, don't forget it was you who failed to make sure she'd stay put at Lucy's when you had the chance. Chew on that while you think about what may happen if she meets up with that forty-five."

NINETEEN: *11:34 P.M.*

Patrolman Cassiday had been a full-fledged member of the Miami Police Force less than a month. He was a well-set-up young man who filled out his new uniform snugly. A veteran of the Korean War who had rebelled against the humdrum of a garage mechanic's job after coming back, he was pleased with his new job and extremely proud to wear the uniform and to wield the authority that went with it.

Cassiday's beat was Miami's Bayfront Park. He walked the winding, palm-shaded paths in steady strides, chin up and eyes alert for any sort of mischief a policeman should put a stop to.

It was like walking a guard post in the army, and snatches from the General Orders often fled through his mind as he paced along:

"To walk my post in a military manner ... always on the alert ... that takes place within sight or hearing. ..."

Of course there was nothing much of a criminal nature taking place in the well-lighted park at night, and that's why a rookie cop always drew the beat. But you never knew, Cassiday kept telling himself sternly. Anything could happen in the park at any time.

Those two men with their heads close together on the bench around the turn—they might be desperate gunmen checking their final plans for holding up the First National Bank in the morning. That blowsy old woman who tottered in front of him, wheezing as she walked and leaving a thick smell of stale beer behind her—what if that were a clever disguise to throw off suspicion while she carried out her cunning plan for kidnaping the mayor's young daughter whom she had lured into the park on some pretext?

In the meantime, until some of these hoped-for events happened, the young patrolman strode his post sternly and alertly, secretly amused to see the way young couples sprang apart at his approach, began talking loudly about inconsequentials, pretending not to notice his uniform as he passed, then melted back into one solid lump in the shadowy darkness behind him as soon as he was ten paces away.

In the beginning, less than a month ago, Cassiday had paused often in his patrol to speak gruffly to such young couples, who hung their heads in abashed silence at his tone. Innocent love-making on a park bench was all right, and he had orders it was to be tolerated up to a point, but how was a young patrolman to know when that point was reached? It was safer by far, he had judged sternly, to nip such little affairs in the bud with a word of warning before they had a chance to go too far.

But that was weeks ago. Before he had met Ann Schwartz. Now he walked his beat as alertly as before, but with much more tolerance for the kisses and caresses under a Miami moon.

Ann Schwartz was a dark little Jewish girl, with elusive laughing eyes, lush breasts and a softly yielding body. He had first met her at a party at his brother-in-law's house two weeks before, and from that day onward his thoughts were all of Ann as he walked the park at night.

Sure she was Jewish, but so what? he argued happily with himself. She didn't really take her religion seriously. She wasn't kosher. She ate bacon with her eggs just the same as any good Catholic, and seemed to have a real yen for all kinds of shell fish.

That kind of Jewish didn't matter if a couple were in

love. And he and Ann were. They had decided that the
second night he dated her. She wasn't any more wrapped
up in her religion than he was in his. A man could go to
Mass occasionally, he thought, and his wife could go to
a synagogue. Why not? At home it wouldn't matter. Not
after the lights were out at night and a man was in bed
with Ann.

Tolerance, that's what the world needed more of, he
told himself wisely, looking the other way as he saw a dark
mass off on the grass beneath a coconut palm writhe in a
peculiar fashion. Three weeks ago he would have halted
and rapped out a stern warning that would have brought
the shame-faced young couple to their feet and out of the
park in a hurry, but tonight he looked the other way and
even smiled foolishly as he thought how it would be to
writhe in the grass beneath a palm tree with Ann.

Not that she was that sort of girl at all. Not with any
fellow except the man she was going to marry. But how
did he know that couple back there weren't engaged, too?
So, why should he interfere?

He pushed his peaked cap back on his forehead as he
strode on, looking upward at the faint moon and feeling
a great warmth of youth and vitality in his loins. Tomorrow was his night off and he was going to her home in
Coral Gables to meet her family. He wasn't worried about
the meeting. He felt he knew them already from Ann's
ready descriptions of them. He would wear his new double-
breasted orlon suit, he decided, with a white shirt and
maybe a black tie to give the right sort of impression
of sober conventionality in front of her parents.

The rippling water of Biscayne Bay was silver in the
faint moonlight on his left through gaps in the shrubbery.
Farther out, he could dimly see the riding lights of a few
yachts anchored in the bay.

He turned sharply away, threading between double
rows of palms whose fronds met over his head, heading

westward now toward the end of his beat where there was a call-box for his hourly report.

He slowed his pace sharply as he followed the heavily shrouded path. He hadn't learned yet to curb his pace so he would come out on time at the call-box. The beat had been laid out for older muscles than his, and he always started out taking it slow and deliberate, but, when his thoughts turned to Ann, his stride quickened unconsciously and he was always getting ahead of himself like this.

He was passing the bench without noticing the figure huddled on it when the toe of his shoe struck something in the path. There was a tinkling sound in the gravel off to the side where his foot had kicked the object, and he stopped and thumbed his flash on to turn a circle of light downward.

The beam first picked out a gold lipstick and then a small hand mirror. Beyond them lay a lady's handbag, gaping open. He swung the light back swiftly and something gleamed wetly on the edge of the path beneath the bench.

The beam came up and he saw the girl lying there. The pallid face and sightless eyes, the gaping wound in her soft throat from which the red wetness beneath the bench had come.

He stood stricken and unable to move for at least twenty seconds. Time enough for the thought to flash through his mind that the dead girl was no older than Ann, and might well have been as pretty as she before the deadly knife had done its work.

Then awareness came to him, and he plunged headlong toward the call-box under the street light.

TWENTY: *11:38 P.M.*

The report reached Will Gentry in his office just as he concluded reminding Shayne that if anything happened to the girl he had sent to Lucy's, it would be the detective's fault because he hadn't mentioned her whereabouts in time.

The inter-com buzzed, and Gentry leaned forward to hear the voice issuing from it.

"Murdered girl in park near Second Street and Second Avenue. Reported by Cassiday on beat. Throat is cut."

Gentry jerked his head up to glare at Shayne. "So it wasn't a forty-five after all. Another knife job."

Shayne was already moving toward the door, and Gentry hurried after him. "You don't know it's the same girl," Shayne flung over his shoulder angrily.

"I'm betting," Gentry challenged him grimly. "You want to risk any dough on it?"

Shayne snorted loudly and went out the side door to his parked car.

He gunned it away fast, but by the time he reached the intersection an ambulance and two radio cars were already there. Spotlights made dazzling bright the cluster of men gathered about a park bench forty feet down the path.

Shayne pulled in behind the ambulance and got out. He stood for a moment beside his car as though nerving himself for the ordeal, then strode slowly down the path, his face set and expressionless.

Three policemen standing in front of the bench looked

at him silently and drew back a little as he walked up. A white-coated ambulance attendant knelt beside the bench.

Shayne peered over his shoulder and saw the girl's face. He was steeled for the shock and there was only a faint grimace on his trenched face as he recognized her.

He stepped back and asked gruffly, "How long ago, Doc?"

The kneeling intern shrugged and answered without looking up. "An hour maybe."

"You got anything on it, Shayne?" one of the officers asked, but Shayne turned away without answering him as Gentry hurried up the path.

The police chief looked at him questioningly, and Shayne nodded and said stiffly, "I'm glad I didn't put up any money."

Gentry's eyes probed at his face for a moment, then he nodded and stepped past him to confer with the young patrolman who had discovered the body.

Shayne walked on a few feet and stopped to lean his right shoulder against the smooth round trunk of a palm. He got out a cigarette and lighted it, controlling the shaking of the match so it was hardly noticeable. He drew in a deep lungful of smoke and expelled it slowly, and his body seemed to slouch negligently against the palm as though he had no interest at all in the scene behind his back.

He stayed that way and didn't turn around until Gentry called to him sharply. "Shayne! Take a look at this."

He took a last drag of smoke and spun his cigarette away, turned to see the chief holding a sheet of paper in his hands.

"It is Nellie Paulson after all. Here's a receipted bill from the Hibiscus for last week's rent on room three-sixteen. And there's some other stuff in her handbag. It's Nellie all right."

Shayne strode back savagely. "It can't be. We had it

worked out that it had to be the Barnes girl."

"Take another look at her," invited Gentry. "You sure she's the one that—"

"Good Christ! Of course I'm sure," burst out Shayne. "I don't need another look. So she's Nellie Paulson. And the same job has been done on her as on the one that came out of the bay. Barnes or Paulson. God knows. Where does this leave us?"

"Pretty damn well up the creek without a paddle," said Gentry savagely. "Two in one night. Goddamn it, Shayne—"

Shayne was looking at him coldly, a muscle twitching in his tight jaw. "And this one right near my hotel, too?" he asked mockingly. "All right. I'd say it looks as though she tried to come back for some more protection from me."

"Yeh," grunted Gentry. "You took the words right out of my mouth. Getting so it's kind of risky being a client of yours, don't you think?"

Shayne said, "You can't say anything I'm not thinking, Will. So let's go on from there."

"Where?" asked the chief sarcastically.

"Well, now we know who she is anyhow. That gives us something more definite to work on."

"Tough way of getting a positive identification. If we wait long enough, maybe we'll stumble over a few more bodies and get *them* identified. Then we may be able to figure it out. That your idea of handling it?"

Strain deepened the trenches in Shayne's cheeks at the chief's tone of acid sarcasm. He said quietly, "Right now I'm wondering why an ex-G.I. with a forty-five under his belt uses a knife instead of the gun."

"For one thing it's a little bit quieter. Let's say he just carries the gun along to frighten private detectives with so they let him walk out into the night to kill off their clients."

"Let's say that," Shayne agreed flatly. He hesitated, rubbing his jaw, moving off the path to let stretcher-bearers from the ambulance go past. "I'd like to get the maid over from the Roney to look at both of them and see if either one are the persons who have been living there as Charles and Mary Barnes."

"Oh, we'll pin down an identification all right," said Gentry bitterly. "As fast as they get killed off, we'll find out who they are."

Shayne continued to disregard his tone. "One thing you didn't get around to telling me back in the office, Will. Did the dead man's fingerprints check with the set in three-sixteen?"

"What? Oh, that. Yes. He's definitely been in three-sixteen since the maid cleaned the room in the middle of the afternoon."

Shayne sighed and started down the path toward his car. Will Gentry clumped along silently behind him. At the sidewalk, Shayne stopped and said, "Let's save the hard feelings until this is over, huh?"

Gentry unexpectedly stuck out his hand. He said, "Sure. Then I'm going to pull your license."

"I think maybe I'll turn it in without waiting for you to pull it, Will." Shayne took his hand absently and without much vigor. "They found no weapon, huh?"

Gentry shook his grizzled head. "Almost exactly the same sort of wound as the other. One fast slash with a hell of a sharp knife. You got *any* ideas, Mike?" The question was almost an entreaty.

"Only one and it's not much good. Something I should have done before. You still got that picture I gave you at the morgue?"

"It's back in my office."

Shayne said, "If you're going back now, I'll pick it up."

TWENTY-ONE: *10:47 P.M.*

Driving away from the Hibiscus Hotel, Bert Paulson's scarred face was dark and scowling as he slumped behind the wheel, scarcely noticing where he was going.

Where to now? What the hell *had* happened to Nellie? Everything was so mixed up, his mind was in a whirl as he considered all the possibilities.

That story the red-headed private detective had told him? How much was fact and how much was lies?

That elevator boy at the Hibiscus! Could he identify him? Place him upstairs on the third floor about the time a disappearing body was being reported as having been seen in 316?

Fear and fierce impatience surged through Paulson's body. The weight of the .45 against his left groin felt good. He wanted to take hold of things with his two hands and tear them apart. Somewhere in this darkened city, Nellie was hiding out from him. Hiding from him in an agony of fear that he might trace her down.

Well, she had every right and reason to be hiding out from him. If he did manage to get his hands on her—

His big hands tightened on the steering wheel and the battle scar from Korea stood out whitely on his cheek as anger raged inside him.

It was his responsibility. The whole sorry affair was his doing. If he'd only realized sooner what Nellie was getting herself into—

The neon lights of a restaurant and bar reminded him that he had not eaten since that afternoon. He pulled into the curb sharply and got out. With a couple of drinks and some food, he might be able to think things out a little more clearly. Driving aimlessly around the streets like this was no good. That damned redhead had probably already reported to the police that he'd walked out on him flourishing a gun and swearing to find Nellie. They'd have a description of him—

He went into a long, low room with a curved bar directly beyond the entrance, tables and booths on his right. It was fairly well crowded and not too well lighted. A haze of smoke added to the dimness.

Half a dozen men were seated on leather stools at the bar, and three-quarters of the tables were occupied by couples and groups of three or four, laughing over drinks or eating late dinners.

Paulson strode down the line of booths and found an empty one near the end. He slid into it so the scar on his face was toward the wall, and he was careful to keep the other side toward the waitress when she arrived almost immediately and asked in a somewhat disapproving tone, "Are you alone, sir?"

"Yes." His voice was surly, demanding to know what of it.

She said brightly, "Then perhaps you wouldn't mind moving to one of the smaller tables. We like to keep the booths free for larger parties."

He wanted to shout at her that he'd be damned if he'd move out to one of the tables where he could be observed by everyone. That he was a paying customer and just as good as anyone else in the joint, and he'd damned well occupy a booth if he wanted to.

But fear and worry about Nellie were slowly teaching him caution, and he restrained himself to say, "As a matter of fact, another couple are meeting me for dinner a little later. I'll have a couple of drinks while I wait."

"Yes, sir. Of course in that case— What would you like

to drink?"

"Canadian rye and water. A double with water on the side." He sat back and lit a cigarette as she went away. By God, he needed a drink. A couple of fast doubles. That was the ticket. Then he'd settle down to some hard thinking. Right now he felt almost giddy. There was a nightmarish quality about the events of the evening that gave him a gnawing sense of sickness in his belly. He was beginning to think he hadn't played it very smart with Michael Shayne. Either should have played along with the guy—gained his confidence and got his co-operation in looking for Nellie—or else he should at least have slugged the redhead before going out as he did.

The waitress came with a double shot-glass full to the brim with whisky, and a glass of ice water. Paulson lifted the smaller glass avidly and drank from it, held his breath while he seized the water and took a big swallow. His throat burned a trifle and warmth crept into his stomach. The whisky was raw and strong. He took another sip and then a larger drink of water, poured the rest of the liquor into the larger glass and sloshed it around with the water. It was too weak to do much good when he tasted it, and he turned to watch through the opening into the booth for his waitress. When he caught her eye he held up two fingers, nodding toward the glass in his hand.

She came with another double shot, and he dribbled all of it into the water glass.

Now the drink was just right. Wonderful. Magnificent. It didn't burn his throat, but it had authority. It was beginning to dissolve the gnawing knot in his belly.

He knew, now, that it had been a bad mistake not to have slugged Shayne. He could have done it easy enough, and goddamn it, he would have enjoyed slugging the big bastard. Tough guy, huh? Well, none of them were so very tough after they got slugged by Bert Paulson.

The way he had sat around and kept Paulson talking

about Nellie when all the time he had the girl hidden in his kitchen! Damn his soul. So now Nellie was gone and only God knew where she was. Or what she was doing.

He drank more of the blended whisky and water, and the knot went away altogether. Suddenly his glass was empty except for two half-melted ice cubes. He frowned and caught the waitress's attention, and told her somewhat thickly, "Another dose of the same, Miss. Guess my friends are held up."

She said something about that was too bad, and went away to bring him another double Canadian rye with more water on the side.

He kept hold of his first glass when she returned, poured the whisky on top of the ice and then carefully measured water in to exactly the proper combination. Not too strong to go down easily, not so weak that you couldn't feel it hit bottom.

Having contrived exactly the right strength, he sipped the mixture happily. Let's see now. He was going to do some straight thinking. That was it. Those two doubles had fixed him up just fine. The thing was, now, to keep up just the right edge. Because now his mind was fine and clear. He was in just the right mood to out-think Mike Shayne and all the cops in Miami. It was like being back in Korea. Out-thinking the enemy. He'd always been good at that. He was alive, wasn't he? And a lot of the damned yellow Communists were dead. Why? Just because he'd out-thought and out-fought 'em, by God!

So he could do it again. Just him against all of them. What the hell did the odds matter? Hadn't he been up against worse odds in Korea?

As the level of liquid receded in the glass, it was like he had been a one-man army in Korea. Like he had de-feated the enemy single-handed. There had been other American soldiers around, of course, but he had really done the worst of the job. He was Bert Paulson, wasn't he?

Well, wasn't he? he demanded fiercely of himself. Things were beginning to get a little mixed up in his mind again. *He* wasn't in the Hibiscus Hotel with his throat cut, was he? Then who in hell said he was? Somebody had.

Nellie! That was it. Or else the redhead was lying. That was a lot more likely. Hell! Why hadn't he caught on that was it right away? Damned foolishness to think Nellie had seen him there with his throat cut. Nellie knew better than that. She knew her own brother, didn't she?

Well, *didn't* she?

He finished his third drink and gravely debated having another. Reluctantly, he decided against it. He was feeling fine, now. Wonderful. Just had a little edge on. Just right for the things he had to do.

And he didn't want any food. That was always a mistake—eating after drinking. Food just absorbed the liquor in your belly and sobered you up.

No more drinks. No food. This was just right.

He got out his wallet and fumbled in it. The waitress saw him and came to his booth with a slip of paper on a small, round tray. She asked brightly, "Stood you up, I guess?"

He blinked at her, wondering what she meant. Then he remembered about the couple he'd invented who had been supposed to meet him for dinner. He said thickly, "Guess so. Haven't time to wait any longer."

He peered near-sightedly at the bill. Damn that accident that broke his glasses. He'd have to get another pair. First thing in the morning. Too late to do it tonight, he guessed. Goddamned lazy opticians probably all closed up shop when it got dark.

The figures on the slip swam before his gaze and he asked the waitress, "How much?"

She told him and he blinked down at his wallet and carefully selected a five. He put it on her tray and said, "Keep change."

When she had gone away, he got up stiffly and slid out, walked a little unsteadily to the front door, remembering to keep the left side of his face averted as he passed the bar and went out into the cool night.

Things blurred as he dragged in a lungful of the clean air. He staggered a little more obviously as he went to his car and got under the wheel.

Looking for Nellie. That's what. Had to find her.

He put the car in gear and it lurched away. Lessee, now. Where was he exactly? He didn't know Miami too well, but it is an easy town for a stranger to orient himself in if he can read street signs, and he paused at the next intersection to peer out the windshield and read them aloud.

Sure. He knew now. Turn to the left and drive about six blocks. Then to the right three blocks. That was it.

Everything was all right now. He knew exactly where he was and where he was going. He needed another little night-cap maybe. Then he'd sleep soundly. And first thing tomorrow he'd get some new glasses and then he'd find Nellie.

The Silver Glade was a modest night-spot in the Southwest section not more than ten blocks from Michael Shayne's hotel. It had a floor show and a small dance floor, and it served honest drinks of liquor to natives or to tourists sober enough to notice what they were drinking.

Because it was close and because the bartender knew Shayne's preference in cognac, the detective was in the habit of dropping into the Silver Glade occasionally for a late drink. When he entered the door tonight the hat-check girl smiled at him brightly and said, "Long time no see, Mr. Shayne," as she took his Panama without bothering to give him a check for it.

She was a big-breasted girl wearing an evening gown that had been carefully cut to accentuate her bigness. Shayne leaned on the low counter in front of her and pleased her by leering at the deep valley beneath her chin and told her, "I can only stand the rot-gut you serve here every so often."

He took the four-by-six photograph from his pocket and pushed it in front of her. "For a well-stacked doll, I always figured you were pretty smart. Ever see this guy around?"

She giggled appreciatively and gave her body a little shake to pull the low-cut gown a little lower. "Always kiddin', aren't you?" She leaned forward so he could get a better look, and studied the picture doubtfully.

"Don't remember as I have. You know how it is. Half the time I don't even look at them when I hand out checks—unless they're big, ugly redheads, that is."

Shayne said, "Try hard. This evening is what I want. Last two or three hours."

"I swear I can't say. It sure doesn't ring any bell." Shayne nodded and turned, bringing his elbow up to brush against the distended fullness of her flesh so that she giggled again.

Holding the photograph in his hand, he went to the bar where there was an empty stool at one end. The bartender was middle-aged and bland-faced. When he saw the redhead coming to the bar, he turned and reached up to the top shelf to lift down a bottle of Martell that had an ordinary cork in it instead of the silvered pouring spout in most of the other bottles.

He set it on the bar in front of Shayne and uncorked it with a flourish, provided a four-ounce glass and a tumbler of ice water, and said reprovingly, "Don't see you around much, Mike."

Shayne laid the picture on the counter and poured cognac in the small glass. "You notice this bird in here this evening?"

The bartender looked down at it, then reached into his hip pocket for a pair of glasses in a leather case. He hooked them behind his ears and studied the man's face carefully.

"Can't say that I did, Mike, but that doesn't mean he wasn't in. You know how it is—if a man isn't a steady—"

Shayne said, sure, he knew how it was. He sipped his drink morosely, and a slim, dark man in elegant evening clothes came up behind him and clapped him lightly on the shoulder.

"Glad to see you, Shamus. So long as you're not pinching the joint. On the house, Henry," he told the bartender, nodding toward the bottle.

"Not as long as you put out Martell for free," Shayne told the proprietor pleasantly. He moved the picture back with his forefinger on it. "You had anybody in this evening that looked like this?"

Salvadore studied it critically, twisting his smooth black head slightly to one side.

"Sure. Dozens of them just about like that. He isn't one you'd pick out of a crowd."

"I know. That's the hell of it. This is really very important, Salvadore. Take it around to the waiters and busboys, huh? Make everyone take a long look. If *any* of them think they saw him in here tonight, let me talk to them."

"Sure, Mike." Salvadore Rotiselli took the picture daintily between thumb and forefinger and minced away. Henry had moved down the bar to serve another customer, and Shayne glowered down at his drink.

He hadn't much hope of success with the picture. As Salvadore said, the face was too thoroughly ordinary, too completely undistinguished to give anyone reason for remembering it.

But it was all Shayne had left now. If he could prove the dead man had actually been in the Silver Glade after nine-thirty, it would be a cinch he hadn't gone into Biscayne Bay from room 316 of the Hibiscus.

But what would that prove? Shayne asked himself angrily. Nothing, really. He still wouldn't know the actual identity of the man with the scarred face—nor of the dead man.

Bert Paulson? Charles Barnes? A dead girl in the park. Until he looked at her face and at the receipted bill from the Hibiscus, he had been so dead certain she wasn't Nellie Paulson.

The other identity fitted her so much better. Mary Barnes from the Roney. Mary Barnes, who had caught a fleeting glimpse of her murdered brother after being summoned by him to the Hibiscus. Mary Barnes who had fled in terror from the man with the scarred face—who had sought refuge in his hotel room and then run out into the night still in terror because she did not trust him to protect her from the man she feared.

All those facts fitted what little he knew about Mary and Charles Barnes. They didn't fit what he knew about Nellie Paulson.

He drank his cognac morosely, washing it down with tiny sips of water from the glass while the questions ran around and around and around in his mind.

There was something eluding him. Something important. Perhaps a key to the entire puzzle. Some tiny bit of information he had that he didn't *know* he had.

That wasn't exactly it. He knew it was there. Somewhere in the maze of conflicting stories and reports he had listened to this evening. Something that had seemed wholly irrelevant at the time, yet which might be supremely important.

He doggedly went over and over again in his mind every single thing that had happened since the telephone call had taken him from Lucy's side.

It was there. He knew it was. Hidden away in his subconscious. He had no idea what it was nor how to go about searching among the half-truths and irrelevancies to dig it out.

Yet it had to come. He had a feeling that time was running out. He glanced down at his watch, wondering absently why he felt that way. While the girl had been missing from Lucy's—before her body had been found in the park —it was natural that he had felt fiercely he must find her before something happened.

But that was over now. The pressure was off. She was dead and no power on earth could make that part of it right again. He had let her slip away from his apartment— had stood supinely by while a man with a .45 walked out to look for her—had cleverly concealed her whereabouts from Will Gentry because he had felt capable of handling the thing himself.

For those reasons, she was dead. Why did he feel time

was running out now?

His watch said 11:46.

And then he knew suddenly. Fourteen minutes to midnight. He had promised Lucy, that was it. That he'd be back by midnight for the drink she had poured out for him.

Salvadore came up beside him and laid the photograph down with a sigh. "No soap, Shamus. Not one of them will say positively yes or no."

Shayne looked down at the picture wonderingly. As though he had never seen it before. Because now it didn't matter. Because now he knew what had been nagging at him.

He slid off the stool without even thanking Salvadore, went toward the door in long strides, his face bleak with anger at his own stupidity.

He didn't hear the check girl call out to him as he stormed past her. He broke into a trot as he went out the door, ran to his parked car and jerked the door open. A moment later it was roaring away from the curb.

TWENTY-THREE: *11:47 P.M.*

The Tropical Arms Hotel on North Miami Avenue was located between a liquor shop and a delicatessen. The liquor store was still open when Shayne pulled up in front of the hotel and leaped out.

The Tropical Arms was an old hotel, very much gone to seed. There was a big, empty lobby with shabby, rococo decorations, yawning chairs and wilted potted palms.

A drop-light over the desk was the only illumination, and there was no one behind the desk.

A hand-printed card propped against a mechanical push-bell instructed Shayne to "Ring for service."

He hit the button sharply with his palm and a loud, metallic "ping" echoed through the empty lobby. Nothing happened, and he kept on pinging until a door opened in a side wall behind the desk and a fat man in his shirt-sleeves emerged. He had pouting lips and he smelled strongly of gin as he waddled up to the desk and grunted, "I heard you the first time, Mister. No need to wake up all the guests."

Shayne skipped the obvious retort. He demanded, "Do you have a Miss Paulson?"

"*Miss* Paulson?" The fat man belched as he shook his head. "No siree, we sure don't."

"Mr. Paulson? *Bert?*"

"Well, yes, now. Mr. Paulson is with us for a fact."

"Since when?"

"Just this evening checked in. Not more'n an hour ago."

"What's his room number?"

"Well, I'll tell you, Mister. You wanta talk to Mr. Paulson, I reckon—"

"What number?" Shayne's voice rasped like a file on tempered steel.

"Two-ten. But I'm trying to tell you—"

Shayne turned away fast and went past the closed door of an elevator to stairs on one side. He climbed two flights and found 210. He knocked loudly and tried the door. It was locked and his knocking brought no response.

He cursed at the delay, studied the lock as he got a ring of keys from his pocket. The lock yielded to the first key he chose. Shayne flung the door open on a lighted bedroom. He stood glaring at the huddled figure of a man on the floor beside the bed. An Army automatic lay on the floor beside him. But there was no smell of gun-powder in the tightly closed room.

Shayne pulled the door shut and walked over to look down at the man with the scarred face. His cheeks were very red and his mouth was open and he breathed stertorously. Just beyond his right hand lay a corked pint bottle of whisky about a quarter full.

Shayne leaned over and shook him roughly, calling, "Paulson! Wake up, Paulson," in his ear. He got no response.

He stepped back with narrowed eyes and kicked the drunken man hard in the buttocks. There was still no response.

Sighing, Shayne went into the bathroom and turned on the light. There was a rust-stained tub with a shower apparatus on the wall at one end.

He went back and got a grip under Paulson's armpits, dragged him into the bathroom and tumbled him inside the tub. He lay there, an inert mass, still breathing loudly and steadily.

Shayne drew the tattered shower curtain to protect himself from the spray, reached a long arm past it and turned on the cold water.

The spray hit full on Paulson's legs, and Shayne reached up to the adjustable head and moved it so it hit him in the face.

Paulson moaned and feebly lifted one arm to ward off the cold water. Shayne turned it on full force and moved the head slowly, sending the stinging spray up and down the length of Paulson's body.

He twitched and jerked and moaned, then sat up suddenly with his eyes wide, grunting, "I'm drowning. Turn it off, I tell you."

Shayne moved the head so the spray took Paulson squarely in the face. He blinked and shuddered and put his hands up, then squirmed to a kneeling position and turned his back on the tormenting water.

Shayne turned it off and reached in to gather up a handful of Paulson's water-soaked coat between the shoulderblades. He pulled the sodden man upright and slapped him viciously, first on one cheek and then the other.

Paulson cried out in surprise and hurt, then cursed thickly and twisted away.

Shayne let him go and stepped back grimly. Paulson slid to a crouching position, opening and shutting his mouth without uttering a sound, his eyes gleaming madly.

Shayne leaned forward and slapped him again. He asked coldly, "Can you hear me, Paulson? Understand what I'm saying?"

"I'm c-cold. I'm f-freezing."

Shayne said, "To hell with that. Let's see if you can stand up." He got a grip on his arm and heaved. Paulson helped himself a little and made it to his feet. Shayne dragged him over the edge of the tub, gave him a hard shove through the doorway. He staggered and went flat on his face on the bedroom floor.

Shayne followed and rolled him over on his back, jerked him up to a sitting posture. The madness was going out of

Paulson's eyes, being replaced by fear.

Shayne got the whisky bottle and uncorked it. He held it up to Paulson's open mouth and ordered, "Swallow."

Paulson swallowed two gulps. He coughed and retched and then looked up miserably.

"You're Shayne?" His voice was thick but he sounded rational. "Where's Nellie?"

"We'll know after you answer some questions." Shayne moved aside to pick up the .45 automatic. He stood over Paulson with the heavy weapon negligently in his hand. "Hesitate just once," he said pleasantly, "and I'll break this over your head. Now then. When you reached Jacksonville from Detroit, you found your sister gone. Is that right?"

Paulson nodded dumbly.

"And you nosed around and discovered she had run out on a badger game rap that she'd been pulling with some guy who she pretended was her brother. Right?"

Again, Paulson nodded. He looked down and his fingers scrabbled for the whisky bottle where Shayne had dropped it on the floor. He got it to his mouth with difficulty and drained it. Then he threw it away and put his hands in front of his face and said brokenly, "My fault. All my fault. If I hadn't gone off and left her alone—"

"Shut up and listen to me," said Shayne inexorably. "While you were away, she'd been living with some man and passing him off as her brother. Who was he?"

"Don' know." Paulson's head weaved from side to side. "I don' know. Hired detective to find her. Then I came here—"

"And had a car accident and broke your glasses as you neared Miami," Shayne filled in for him. "You had your sister's room number, and when you reached the Hibiscus you went straight up. And you saw this blonde come running out of her room and you thought it was Nellie afraid to face you because of what she'd done, although you actually couldn't recognize her in that dim light without your glasses."

"Was Nellie," Paulson insisted stubbornly. "I tol' you—"

"I know what you told me," Shayne cut him off fiercely. "If you'd come clean in the beginning and told me it *wasn't* her brother who'd been living with her in Jacksonville, a hell of a lot of things would be different right now. Including one dead girl who might well still be alive."

"Nellie?" Paulson cringed away from Shayne's hard-hitting words. "You mean she's dead? My little sister?"

"Frankly," said Shayne, "I don't know who's dead at this point. But we're going to find out. Get on your feet and let's go to headquarters."

"Can't stand up," groaned Paulson, sinking back on his elbows. "Gotta—be sick."

"Then get the hell in the bathroom and be sick." Shayne stood back and swung a number twelve shoe. The toe of it crunched into Paulson's ribs.

He grunted with pain and rolled over and was sick on the floor.

Shayne stood back, gimlet-eyed and restless, until the retching subsided somewhat. Then he reached down and hauled Paulson up impatiently, half-marched him and half-supported him to the door. Little puddles of water and a pile of foul vomit lay on the floor behind them as they went out.

TWENTY-FOUR: *11:53 P.M.*

Chief of Police Will Gentry was deep in conversation with a tall blond man when Shayne unceremoniously shoved the hulking bedraggled figure of Bert Paulson into his office at headquarters.

Gentry looked up disapprovingly, and then his eyes widened as he saw the scar on Paulson's cheek. He said, "So you found him, Mike? What the hell have my men been doing?"

Shayne said wearily, "I had the jump on them. It finally came to me that he mentioned he and his sister had always stayed at the Tropical Arms when they were in Miami." He jerked his thumb savagely toward Paulson who had subsided into a chair and sat there with a vacant expression on his face. "Meet Bert Paulson in the flesh, Will."

"You're wrong, Mike." Gentry shook his head and turned to the man seated beside him. "Meet Lieutenant Neils from Jacksonville. Mike Shayne. He brought down a picture of the girl and her brother." He gestured toward a blown-up eight-by-ten photograph lying on his desk. "Looks a lot more like the bird we pulled out of the bay than this guy."

Shayne leaned over his shoulder and studied the picture of a smiling girl and a young man in bathing suits with their arms intertwined about each other. The man whom he had dragged out of the Tropical Arms definitely did not resemble the one in the picture. He couldn't be so sure about the girl. The sun was in her face and she was squinting as she smiled and her image was blurred a trifle.

Shayne said flatly, "I realize that's the guy you're after, Lieutenant, but you're mistaken thinking his name is Paulson. Bert will tell you the whole story," he went on impatiently to Gentry. "Right now, I want to know just one little thing. That girl in the park. What sort of purse did she have, Will?"

"Purse?"

"Handbag. You know."

"Hell, it was just a bag, I guess. The kind of bag any girl carries around with her."

"What color?" Shayne demanded savagely. "Red or black?"

Gentry pursed his lips thoughtfully. "I don't know. Come to think of it, I'm not sure I even saw her bag. They had all the stuff out of it looking for identification—"

As he paused uncertainly, Shayne reached past him and snatched up his telephone. He gave Lucy Hamilton's number, and this time she answered before it rang twice.

"Lucy! Think a minute before you answer this. What sort of handbag was the girl carrying when she came to your place?"

"Why—I don't know for sure, Michael. I—"

"I told you to stop and think it over," he exploded. "Was it red or black? Damn it, you ought to remember a simple thing like that. Start thinking about it while I'm on my way over."

"Don't you dare come here at this time of night, Michael. I won't let you in if you do. I'm going to get some sleep. As far as the bag goes, it was black suede. Good *night*."

Her voice rang in his ears for seconds after he heard the decisive slam of her receiver breaking the connection.

He replaced the phone slowly, shaking his head and glancing at his watch. It was still five minutes to midnight. What the hell had got into Lucy?

He straightened his shoulders and told Gentry absently,

nodding toward Paulson, "He's all yours, Will. He'll explain all about the guy Lieutenant Neils has got staked out as Paulson." There was a curious look of concentration on his face as he turned to go out.

"Hold it, Mike. Where you going now?"

"I've got a date with Lucy," Shayne said over his shoulder without slacking pace. "Promised her I'd be back by midnight to have a night-cap with her."

He was out the door without bothering to close it, and he lengthened his stride almost to a run down the corridor and out the side door.

It was something like sixteen blocks from police headquarters to Lucy's apartment, and Shayne covered the distance in something like sixty seconds.

He cut his motor off while swinging into the block that held her apartment building, cut off his lights and slid silently to a stop directly across the street.

The curtains were drawn at her front windows, but edges of light showed around them.

Shayne got out and closed the car door quietly, crossed the street to the foyer and went in.

He had a key on his ring that opened both the downstairs inner door and also her apartment. Lucy had given it to him more than two years before all tied up with a pink ribbon, making a laughing ceremony out of it and jesting about the depravity of a girl who gives her employer a private key to her apartment.

Shayne had been touched by the gift, and he had been very careful never to use it. He had a special signal he always rang on her bell from the foyer so she would know who was calling.

Tonight, he didn't ring her bell. He got out his keys and picked out the shiny new one that had never been used, and carefully inserted it in the lock.

It turned easily and he went in.

He climbed the one flight of stairs slowly and cautiously,

testing each tread for squeaks before putting his weight on it.

At the top, he stopped in front of Lucy's door and drew in a deep breath. Sweat beaded his corrugated forehead and crept down the trenches in his cheeks.

He still held the shiny new key in his hand. He stooped in front of the door and put his left hand on the lock, with thumb and forefinger pressed loosely together in front of the opening to make a sheath of flesh through which he inserted the key without the slightest scraping sound.

When it was firmly bedded, he transferred his hand to the door-knob and pulled on it firmly while he turned the key. Thus, there was no sudden click to betray him when the catch was released.

He turned the knob, keeping pressure on it, and then went into the apartment in a violent lunge.

He caught one fleeting glimpse of Lucy seated in a chair beside the telephone as he went by, but his attention was centered on the other occupant of the room.

Female and blonde and deadly, she sprang from the sofa to meet his rush, and there was the reddish gleam of dried blood on the short-bladed knife in her hand.

Shayne went under the vicious arc of the knife and hit her brutally in the bosom with his shoulder and the full weight of his charging body.

The impact slammed her back against the wall with a crash and she sank to the floor in an unconscious heap.

TWENTY-FIVE: *Midnight*

Shayne wasted one brief look at her face to assure himself that it was the girl with the red patent-leather bag who had thrust Charles Barnes's picture in his pocket in the lobby of his hotel earlier, and that she wouldn't be using her knife again for some time to come.

Then he turned to Lucy with a reassuring grin.

Her ankles and her right arm were bound tightly to the legs and arm of her chair with wide strips of cloth that had been torn from a sheet. Her other hand had been left free so she could lift the telephone receiver behind her. Her face was white with strain and her eyes had a glassy look, but she managed to twist her lips in a feeble smile and to ejaculate with spirit:

"It's about time you were coming to the party."

"Sorry I cut it so fine, angel." Shayne picked up the blood-stained knife from the floor and went to her to kneel and slash her bonds. "You all right?"

"Sure. Just perfect. Aside from my heart being permanently lodged where my adam's apple used to be and a few minor things like that. She's insane, Mike! She's already killed two people with that knife tonight. She boasted about it to me. And she was going to cut my throat, too, just as soon as she got the call she was waiting for. She told me just how she was going to do it—and she giggled while she told me."

Shayne rocked back on his heels and looked up at her sharply. "What call was she waiting for?"

"Some man she called Lanny. He's in cahoots with her

and pretends to be her brother. She left word two places for him to call here the moment he came in. That's all she was waiting for. So she could arrange to meet him. And she let me keep on living so I could answer the phone if you or Will or anybody called in the meantime and tell you not to come here."

Shayne cut the last strip of cloth binding Lucy's wrist, and she stood up, wincing with pain as she rubbed circulation back into her arm.

He lifted the phone and dialed the number that was a direct line to Will Gentry's office, and when the chief's gruff voice answered, he said wearily:

"Come around to Lucy's place to pick up your killer. Nellie Paulson. But do this first. Put a fast tap on Lucy's phone and stake this place out. Nellie's accomplice is supposed to call here any moment. When he does, Lucy will try to stall him long enough for you to trace it—or get him to come here, if she can. You got that?"

"Nellie Paulson?" said Will Gentry. "I thought—"

"Save it until you get that tap fixed and get up here. She spilled the whole story to Lucy."

He hung up and turned to look at Lucy who had limped across the room and was now seated at the end of the sofa in front of the low table holding the liquor tray. Nellie Paulson still lay in an unconscious heap against the wall beyond the sofa. She hadn't stirred since she crumpled to the floor there.

The cognac bottle still stood on the tray, and the glass of brandy Lucy had poured out for Shayne two hours previously was still standing full to the brim.

He looked at his watch and grinned wryly as he went to the chair beside the sofa. "Sorry I didn't quite make it by midnight for that drink, angel."

She shuddered, but kept her tone as light as his. "What made you come at all? I knew she'd cut my throat happily if I said one word over the telephone to indicate what was going on."

"I came because it still lacked five minutes of midnight when you told me I shouldn't dare come here at that hour —that you wouldn't let me in if I did. I knew you too well to believe you wouldn't give me that last minute to keep my promise in—and suddenly everything clicked into place. I knew the murderer was Nellie Paulson and that she hadn't left your place at all. And I still needed this drink," he ended simply, reaching for it and lifting it in the air in a silent toast to his secretary.

Her aplomb exploded suddenly in great racking sobs. "It was terrible, Mike. Just horrible. She told me every single ghoulish detail after she got started. About killing a man named Charlie Barnes in her hotel room after he balked about being shaken down in the badger game she was working with Lanny who has been living with her in Jacksonville as her brother."

"Was she in the room when Barnes's sister looked in and saw Charles dead on the bed?"

"Yes. She hid in the bathroom. She told me all about it, giggling as though it was a big joke. How she wound his coat about his throat so the blood wouldn't spill out, and pushed him out the window into the bay and then ran out and up two flights of stairs and down the elevator without anyone noticing her."

"One of the things I don't get is how she came to be in my hotel lobby waiting for me with a picture of Barnes when I got there."

"She told me all that, too. After she left the hotel, she walked up the street looking for a cab. She found one two or three blocks away and got in and told him to drive by the Hibiscus, just out of curiosity to see if anything was happening. And just then the man's sister, Mary Barnes, came running out of an alley beside the hotel and stopped the cab to away from a man who was chasing her. And Nellie looked back and saw it was her own brother who lives in Detroit. So she just stayed in the cab and heard the driver recommend you as a detective who might help Mary, and watched her get out at your hotel. She had the driver drop her a few blocks away, and she walked back. She would have gone up to your room and killed Mary right then to get rid of the only witness to the other murder, but the clerk refused to give her your room number."

"So she waited until I got there and gave me that story about Barnes being in the Silver Glade, along with his picture."

"She was furious, she said, when you refused to take her money, and went on upstairs. But she thought anyhow she had sort of fixed up an alibi by making you think Barnes was still alive at the Silver Glade at ten o'clock."

Shayne nodded somberly and refilled his glass. He glanced beyond Lucy and lifted one eyebrow as Nellie stirred slightly on the floor.

"I guess I didn't break her back after all. Did she know her brother also followed me to my place?"

"Yes. She kept hanging around outside in the shadows, hoping Mary would come out and she'd get a chance at her. She saw her brother go in, and later he rushed out and jumped in his car and drove away. Then she left, and Mary came up behind her on the sidewalk and recognized her as the girl who'd been in the cab before. Then she lured Mary into the park and got her to sit on a bench and —and cut *her* throat, too. And Mary had told her about your note and how she was coming here, so she left her bag in the park and took Mary's and caught a cab here and gave me the note. Later, after I'd phoned you to say she'd arrived, she suddenly seemed to realize you might be coming here any moment to talk to Mary.

"That's when she took the knife out of her purse and showed me the blood on it and gloated about how sharp it was and how it just slid through the soft flesh of a throat like a knife through warm butter.

"And she *wanted* to try it on me, Michael. Honestly, she was just dying to. But she wanted to stay here while she tried to locate her Lanny—who had gone out of the Hibiscus room before she killed Charlie Barnes and didn't even know she'd done it—and she knew that if I weren't here to answer the phone when you called, you might get suspicious and come up anyway. So then she tore up a sheet and tied me to the chair and told me she'd love to cut *my* throat and watch *my* blood spurt out if I didn't say exactly what she told me to over the phone."

As though the word were a signal, Lucy's telephone shrilled at that exact moment.

She got up, looking questioningly at Shayne, and he nodded. "Answer it. If it's Lanny, stall him as long as you can. Tell him Nellie's in the bathroom. Get him to hang on if you can. Will *should* have a tap on it by this time."

Lucy picked up the phone and said, "Yes?"

She listened a moment, then nodded to Shayne who was waiting intently. "Yes, she is here and she's been trying to call you. If you could hold on a minute? Well—she's in the bathroom right now. Hold on and I'll get her. I know she's awfully anxious to talk to you."

She put down the telephone, looking at Shayne anxiously.

As he nodded his approval, a scrabbling sound behind him made him swing on his heel.

Nellie Paulson had come back to consciousness enough to have gotten up on her hands and knees. She shrank back and opened her mouth to scream as Shayne turned toward her.

He leaped forward and drove the heel of his palm against her mouth before the sound came out.

Lucy watched transfixed, her own mouth wide open. Shayne whirled and saw her, gestured frantically to the telephone on the table.

She understood the gesture and picked it up, asked sweetly, "Oh— Are you still there? Nellie will be out in just a sec."

She continued to hold the receiver to her ear, and after another thirty seconds her eyes widened at sound of loud voices and a struggle at the other end of the wire.

Then a different voice came to her, "You there, Miss Hamilton? Good work. We got him all right. And tell Mike Shayne that Chief Gentry's on his way up and for him to stay put until the chief gets there."

Lucy replaced the phone and reported the conversation to Shayne. Nellie was sunk back on the floor and lay twisted there, moaning softly with her hands over her face.

Shayne grinned wryly at Gentry's order, and sank back into his chair. "Come over and sit in my lap, angel. I swear I'm *never* going to leave you alone again."

Lucy went to him slowly, and he caught her wrist and pulled her down onto his thighs. She flung her arms about his neck and pressed her face against his chest.

He held her quivering body tightly and said into the mass of brown curls beneath his chin:

"I mean it, Lucy. Right now I really mean it. Hurry up and kiss me before Will walks in and spoils everything."

A NEW MIKE SHAYNE MYSTERY

MURDER BY PROXY

BY Brett Halliday

Two dirty glasses and a half bottle of cheap
bourbon on the table; a rumpled king-sized
bed; an overflowing bedside ashtray.

Shayne picked up a stubbed-out filter tip,
looked at its imprint and wondered if the
wild shade of lipstick came from Ellen Har-
ris's hot little lips . . .

A Dell Book   40c

If you cannot obtain copies of this title at your local
newsstand, just send the price (plus 10c per copy for
handling and postage) to Dell Books, Box 2291, Grand
Central Post Office, New York 17, N.Y No postage or
handling charge is required on any order of five or
more books.